A Treacherous Country

K.M. Kruimink was born in Tasmania and spent most of her childhood in the Huon Valley, with an interlude on the West Coast. After completing a largely ornamental Arts degree at the University of Tasmania, she lived and worked interstate and abroad for several years. Today, she lives once again in the Huon Valley, now with her husband and daughter. *A Treacherous Country* is her first novel.

A Treacherous Country

K.M. KRUIMINK

ALLEN&UNWIN
SYDNEY·MELBOURNE·AUCKLAND·LONDON

First published in 2020

Copyright © K.M. Kruimink 2020

All rights reserved. No part of this book may be reproduced or transmitted in any form or by any means, electronic or mechanical, including photocopying, recording or by any information storage and retrieval system, without prior permission in writing from the publisher. The Australian *Copyright Act 1968* (the Act) allows a maximum of one chapter or 10 per cent of this book, whichever is the greater, to be photocopied by any educational institution for its educational purposes provided that the educational institution (or body that administers it) has given a remuneration notice to the Copyright Agency (Australia) under the Act.

Allen & Unwin
83 Alexander Street
Crows Nest NSW 2065
Australia
Phone: (61 2) 8425 0100
Email: info@allenandunwin.com
Web: www.allenandunwin.com

A catalogue record for this book is available from the National Library of Australia

ISBN 978 1 76087 740 8

Set in 13.2/19 pt Adobe Jenson Pro by Bookhouse, Sydney
Printed and bound in Australia by Griffin Press

10 9 8 7 6 5 4 3 2 1

MIX
Paper from responsible sources
FSC® C009448

The paper in this book is FSC® certified. FSC® promotes environmentally responsible, socially beneficial and economically viable management of the world's forests.

For Omes, and for Mum

You with the look of the lost

HOW CAME I TO A place like this?

What spirit drew me here?

These and other questions perplexed my mind on that day's ride north from town. The clouds drifted and the wind blew, as clouds and wind will do. My breath was white in the cold air, and my horse plodded, and when I threw an apple core, it made a nice arc and subsequently fell upon the earth, just as you might imagine. Why, then, if all around me was evidence of the expected natural laws, did my thoughts not remain inside the privacy of my mind, but instead spike up out of my head and my eyes into points of interrogation? Why did I have the profound conviction that I was on the very brink of some discovery of the utmost strangeness? Why did I feel that in the next moment I should find the woman with the tail of a fish, or the fountain that would give me life eternal, or the sherry that would make me sober?

My Cannibal said he did not know. Perhaps he did not care, sauntering along with his thoughts firmly packed into his skull, impenetrable beneath all the hair.

Every time I blinked my eyes, a sea of huge bodies writhed inside my eyelids. Therefore, I stared hard into the bright sharp air, tears bulging in my eyelashes.

I had seen many animals die, but never a man.

I had never wondered if a person can be measured by an absolute value, or if all our qualities, good and bad, are modulated and by degree. And to what degree I myself achieve goodness, and to what degree I fail.

These were the things I ought to have been making into questions. But the eyes with which we look back upon our lives are clearer than the eyes of the moment, I suppose.

A slow sweep of rain moved over us. Behind it, the sun was weak and distant. The season was mid-winter, they told me, and it was indeed cold, although the month was July. All around were leaves flashing like schools of silver-green fish, on trees whose bark rushed and curled like running water.

Here is another question: can the season truly be called winter, if it is at the wrong time of the year, and the leaves have not fallen? Surely it is not winter, but some other thing entirely! It is not very Scientific to point to one thing and declare, Behold, it is cold, and then to point to another, and say, Behold, this too is cold, and conclude that these two things, which in all other respects may be entirely dissimilar, are necessarily One and the Same, based solely upon temperature! There are many things that are cold and not the same. A snowdrift, the sea, a shudder, a fish, metal, rejection. The Lieutenant-Governor ought to have thought of this, or at least have been told. He was a man of Science, I had heard, abreast with the changing times.

I put this to my Cannibal. He said the days had grown shorter, which is also a characteristic of winter. And that it was a good time to plant cabbages.

Tigris was walking dully, her head down. I had bought her before sunrise that same morning from a German man in a green gabardine coat, who conducted his business in an alleyway behind what he told me was an excellent local brothel. The mysterious light of his Argand lamp and the stench of its black oil had overpowered me, weakened as I was (for I had had no breakfast), and momentarily suspended my knowledge of the buying of horses. And whilst I do not know that any German has heretofore been called exotic, his accent in that moment had struck me as such. It was with a mind thus caught up by these various stupefying influences that I had first beheld the mare, and so she had seemed truly marvellous. She was like a horse cut out of the night sky, throwing a rippling shadow against the brothel's brick wall, gazing beyond me to Elysium with eyes like enormous drops of ink. A Grecian beast, worthy of an Odyssey such as mine!

'Tigris is not a Greek word,' the German had told me. 'The tackle is included in the price,' he had added, casting a searching look along the alleyway, as though he should rather be elsewhere.

I am afraid the animal had grown rather less impressive as the day wore on. There had been a distinct aroma of boot polish about her that morning in the alleyway, which the German had told me was a kind of saddle oil peculiar to the colony. This aroma had caught in my nostrils and troubled me all morning, for I slowly grew to understand it was, in fact, boot polish, as it was gradually rubbed away from certain areas where it had been smeared to hide the horse's bald patches. Now, in the rain, a slow tide of black polish crept inevitably towards my white gaiters. These imperilled items were new; I had purchased them in Sydney-town, and I did not adore the notion that their smart martial look should be besmeared as the result of my own innocence.

For a while this brought me very low, for such deceit was nothing less than cruel Extortion, to my indignant way of thinking. I yearned for Pharaoh, my barely tamed bay stallion at Home. O, for some spirit and a tossing head! I resolved several times over to dismount and set Tigris free, leaving her to wander off into the forest and find the Fountain of Youth and live forever mediocre, locked into the attic of her own mind. For not only was she ugly, but she was also Stupid. I had tried to offer her my apple core, leaning over her neck, but she was so taken aback by my arm appearing before her that all she could manage was an ungainly shuffle in the midst of the road and then to resume her latter plod, ignoring the apple core entirely. As we trudged on, however, the extreme vicissitudes of my feeling eventually found the midpoint where they habitually settle, and I kept the mare with me. She was unimpressive, it was true, but she was a tractable creature. She went forth with dumb conviction, her flanks warm, following my Cannibal along a meditative road overhung with trees.

'Why is she called Tigris?' I had asked the German.

'Because,' he had replied, 'the sire was called Lake Hazar.'

I did not know what that meant, but I did not ask—nor, indeed, did I make any of the usual pertinent enquiries when buying a horse. I paid him the sum he asked without bargaining, although it left me with very little ready money; in short, I paid for gold and got brass.

Leaves like scimitars carpeted the road.

I clanked as I went. My Cannibal, padding along in boots so moulded to his feet he and they had surely been unearthed together at Pompeii, said I was scaring off the birds. Good! What flesh-eating avians must have been lurking in those foreign trees! Tigris had not the wit to be perturbed by the noise. This clanking came from the damned—forgive me—harpoons.

Since Sydney-town, I had borne the burden of two harpoons; the newest Technology, I had been told, American in design, with a single flue and a soft shaft, quite unlike our antiquated English kinds. Whatever the meaning of all that was, I did not know. What did I know of harpoons? God confound Confusion! And God confound the card game in which I had won them. Better that I had lost! For, I had discovered, no one wished to buy American harpoons, and they are jolly cumbersome. Not only this, but they had also served to distract me from my great Purpose there in the colonies.

To look at me, the idle observer would be forgiven for not immediately divining that I was a man with a Grave Mission, as I went along on my stupid horse with my hideous Contraptions of harpoons. And yet it was so.

The invisible flesh-eating birds coughed and cackled from within the trees.

I was tired.

I wished to remain honest.

The previous night, I had got some advice from a sailor which I took rather to heart, because he looked very much like Richard III and had therefore an air of natural authority about him. I cannot recall the name of the public house in which I met him, but I can report it was of dubious cheer, peopled by Specimens of a kind I can hardly describe. It cannot have been more than forty years old, for that was the age of the colony, and yet its beams and boards had the black smoke-and-grog pickling to them that only the inns of greatest antiquity achieve at Home. It was in this institution that I was compelled to secure lodging for myself and my pair of American harpoons, a storm of exceeding inconvenience having descended upon the town as we docked, and the inn being nearest to hand. I had intended to pay a visit to the nearest Bank immediately upon arrival, in order to draw funds against my letter of credit, but the storm had so delayed us that night had fallen when at last I descended to the terra firma of Hobart-town.

I had but little baggage, having been unfortunately divested of many of my trappings in Sydney through a confluence of mischance and my own poor judgement. My reduced accoutrements were now quite manageable by hand for a short distance, even with the harpoons. I put my head down against the torrent and ploughed through the storm towards the dim and oily light of the inn.

My evening there had begun indifferently with a meal of gristle unencumbered by beef and a glass of oleaginous vinegar that could scarcely remember the vineyards of Italy (although it did rather evoke the Mediterranean coast, for there was a kind of gritty stuff collected in the bottom of the cup, like sand). I took this repast at the table nearest the hearth with the harpoons propped beside me, whence they first drew the eye of a Jezebel who approached and asked me in quite an ordinary way why my harpoons had such an odd look about them.

She was young, with interesting dark eyes and a neck so long it looked like she had survived a hanging—perhaps she had. She told me she had worked amongst sailors and whalers for five years and had seen a great deal, but never such queer-looking harpoons. We then embarked upon a very civil conversation on the topic of my harpoons, which expanded into a rumination upon the trade of whaling itself, and did not conclude until the young woman seemed to remember herself and, with a half-heartedness that was not encouraging, offered to meet me in a private place for a certain sum. We were interrupted by the sailor I have mentioned, the one with the look of Richard III, hunchback and all, who hobbled forth to say, 'Sally, be off with you, for this is an honest place.'

'My name is not Sally, Jack.'

'All such girls as this are called Sally,' he said to me.

'And all such men as you are called Jack,' said she to him.

The sailor conceded that he was, in fact, called Jack, and the girl withdrew, telling me she would not stay where she was not welcome, and that her name was Maria Regina, after the Virgin, and went bare-armed and bare-headed out into the storm.

She had seemed perfectly honest to me, and I do not think my own intentions had been dishonourable. It is true that I am quite easily led, and I had enjoyed conversing with a young person with interesting eyes and a half-hanged neck, and who paid me a morsel of attention, for I was quite alone in that place. But I was loyal to my dear Susannah, I told myself, and would be worthy of her.

I carried with me the memory of love as a little shadow in my heart. If I were in a cheerful mood, this shadow of love bolstered me, but when I was downhearted and lonely, it gave me nothing but more questions.

The sailor cast his attention to my harpoons, and briefly I thought I might have found a buyer at last. But to my sorrow, his interest only went so far as to examine and expound upon every flaw in their design.

'Indeed, I am encountering some difficulty in selling them,' I told him.

Leaning against the bar, so as to ease his humped back, he told me that I might divest myself of them for a fair price at a whaling-station, if I were to go in person to visit such a place. There I might find a Customer with the most immediate need and the independence (if an harpooner) to select and purchase his own weapon. He should also have the disposition to do so, if he were employed by a whaling-station that paid a commission, by whale, and I were able to convince the harpooner of the superiority of my devices. That sounds more trouble than it is worth, I said. Yes, it is, said the man. And what is a whaling-station? I asked. He laughed and gave me up for useless—as I certainly was. I paid for his ale.

Before the great burden of the harpoons had come upon me, I would have used this interchange to ask the sailor Richard III if he had any news or knowledge of the woman whom I had travelled across savage oceans from England to rescue. What distraction! Two harpoons and I did not even think to mention her name.

I resolved to do better.

There was a great fireplace in the tap-room with a fire ablaze within, which may sound somewhat like cheer, but, in short, was not. The fire hissed and spat like an indignant Cat from the rain leaking down the chimney, and what little warmth and comfort it may nevertheless have provided was rather dampened by the conceivably human figure piled into a chair before the hearth. This personage's head and face were entirely subsumed by great profusions of perplexing hair and was—the Hair or the Man, or both—emitting a most extraordinary aroma. He so blocked the fire's effects that I remained wet from the storm, although I had been as near the hearth as I could for above two hours. All that reached me was a thick and cloying smoke.

The Person before the fire did also succeed in rather gaining the upper hand—conversationally, I mean—by speaking at all, that being so unexpected from such a Creature. As I withdrew from the sailor, harpoons over my shoulder and gristle in my teeth, the figure in the chair produced a mouth from amongst the hair and said, 'Come now, man, do not look so downcast.'

What can one say to simple kindness from a stranger? It shoots straight to the heart of a vulnerable person.

The fire picked out two twinkling grey eyes amongst his hirsute visage.

'How did you come by those irons?' he asked.

'What irons?' I asked. 'Forgive me, sir, I do not know to what you refer.'

'Your harpoons, man,' he said, with a smile. 'Where did you find them? I find it difficult to imagine that you intentionally have bought them yourself, for—and I hope you will forgive the presumption—you quite clearly have nothing to do with the whaling industry.'

'Ah—yes. As to that, I won them in a card game.'

'Bad luck!'

'Thank you.'

He nodded very civilly. 'There is a commodious whaling-station a day north-east of here,' he continued. 'It is known as the Montserrat Station, and it is renowned for its black oil.'

'Indeed?' I said, for want of something better.

This remark caused the hairy man to smile, though I did not perceive why.

'Indeed. I am employed there, and I will return to-morrow. Why do we not go together, man, and find safety in company on treacherous roads? And when we are there, I will introduce you to Mr Heron, who is the Station-Master, and he will perhaps purchase your irons. Or, if he does not, I shall introduce you to one or another of our harpooners, who may wish to purchase your goods directly—especially young Jackie, who seems to have a head for Technology. At any rate, no matter which person is or is not interested in your harpoons, Mr Heron might perhaps also extend to you an offer you may wish to entertain. That is, you might buy the station yourself, as Mr Heron has an ill wife and wishes to give up the business. He will sell at a loss, I am certain, for his wife will not dwell in Hobart-town without him—she says it is too rough—and so she lives under his protection in a place greatly rougher, which is not conducive to her health, although, in my opinion, the air there is the finest and freshest in the world. And I have breathed the air of ten continents, so I am well placed to make the judgement.'

I did not know if he had forgotten he was addressing me directly, for he was gazing ruminatively into the flames as he spoke, and showed no signs of *not* launching into the story of his life and all his ancestors. The man was Irish, as I determined from his voice, and I did have it upon good authority that the Irish on this Isle were all Cannibals. Although, I must admit, the young Maria Regina with the black eyes had also been Irish, and she had not seemed a flesh-eater. And the Personage before me seemed more and more a Man as he spoke, and less a pile of putrid and hairy rags. He shifted his position, and I saw he had a great canvas sheet about his shoulders, which he dropped to the ground. With this impediment gone, he stood, and presented quite an ordinary appearance, but for the hair, and the bare feet. A pair of bedraggled boots steamed upon the hearth behind him. These contributed, I think, to the general malodour. This olfactory offence lingered, but we are imperfect creatures, we humans, and I forgave.

'I am not in the whaling business, sir,' I said. 'I do not need to buy a station. I do not mind telling you I do not know what a whaling-station is.' True, but I had already begun to form an impression of it in my mind. I had a vision of a great floating Platform, loaded with all manner of tools and supplies, frequented by great whaling-ships, which would moor and be loaded with every necessity before sailing out over the rugged seas upon their hunt.

'Come and see it, sir, and you may find yourself convinced.'

'You say this station of yours is a day north of here—by what means? By boat?'

'Yes, if you have enough men to row, but I do not. I had intended to walk.'

'I cannot walk so far, with my harpoons, and my things,' I said.

'I know a man who will sell you his horse for a good rate,' said the Irishman.

'Well, besides this, I have business in town, sir. I must visit the Bank.'

'Have you no ready money?'

'Only a modest sum.'

'You will not need any more than that.'

'But you would have me buy a horse! And purchase the station! Surely money is required—although I maintain I have no use for it, nor the funds exactly to spare . . .'

'What, do you think Mr Heron would take cash in hand? It is a large purchase, and would be solemnised here in town, with the participation of—Bankers, and so on.'

'And the horse?'

'Modest horses abound, in this place, for modest sums. The fellow I know will have just the thing.'

'There is something else, and this is the thing we really must consider, for it is more pressing than the—admittedly also pressing—matter that I do not want a horse or a whaling-station. My purpose in Hobart-town is not to sell the harpoons. This matter is entirely peripheral to my true purpose here, which is to find a woman called Maryanne Maginn.'

He repeated the name with a contemplative tone, and said, 'And you are sure she is not at the station, or somewhere along the way there?'

'My friend,' I said, deciding we had conversed long enough, 'I thank you, but I must decline.'

'Aye, that is prudent,' he told me. 'However, I will ask you—you with the look of the lost—whatever shall you do instead?'

You Told Me We Would Be Eaten Alive

THE ROAD NORTH WAS WINDING and beset by hills, which well suited my perturbed spirit. We emerged from the wood and from the rain into a singing land of frosted fields and softly undulating valleys, dense with distant green canopies, all cupped by ancient peaks and ridges. It struck me as quite bewildering that in the southern reaches of the world these hills brooded quietly on over their forested Isle, while farther north the Greeks fell and the Romans rose, and then fell, and before them the Etruscans did whatever they did, and so on and on right up to modern English society. No doubt, too, these southern hills were looked upon by countless generations of Men unknown to the Romans, who perhaps cycled through their own great rising and falling and rising!

One or two lonely wooden farmhouses nestled in the bosom of the fields, but I had not yet seen a soul abroad.

I remarked to my Cannibal that I had not seen a stone house since we had left Hobart-town.

'There are more trees than stones here,' he told me.

'Who counted?'

He laughed. 'An expression, merely,' he said, affecting an accent close to my own, for the sake of comedy, I presumed. 'You will see stone houses by-and-by,' he added.

The air was so clear and thin that I was able to see straight into the kitchens and bedchambers of the farmhouses, and to count the leaves of the trees on the distant hillside. Great shadows of clouds skimmed across the landscape, sliding down the hillsides and rippling over the green. I could count the drops of rain in the clouds themselves. Sheep and cattle ruminated upon the grass, little green circles in the white all around them—hoof-prints in the frost.

So far removed was I then from the stormy passage to the Isle, tossed upon indifferent seas, the foulest human Fluids slick on my boots, and my entry into little Hobart-town under cracking clouds and rain like shards of glass! I could scarcely believe the change a day had brought. I am from the countryside, and it is the place I love, and this place was so very nearly like it. I felt a lifting in my heart, and an emptiness, that I was of no significance at all. And indeed I was not, I the third son, with the pure liberty of he who does not matter.

We passed a graveyard, perched upon a rise as we skirted below. A little island of the lost, for which I could see no attendant church.

'Is that a Church of England graveyard?' I asked.

'I do not know, for there is no church, and I have not been to look at the graves,' said my Cannibal.

'I asked merely with the presumption that you might know because you are acquainted with these parts.'

'Well, it may be Church of England,' he conceded. 'There are many such types who dwell here.'

'Here—in the graveyard?'

'Here—in the valley, man.'

'I imagine you are not amongst this number.'

'Certainly not. I do not dwell here, but farther north, and to the east.'

'That was not my meaning, sir.'

'You meant I am not Church of England? Why ought I be? Foreign institution that it is!'

Why had I asked? Of course the man was not Church of England. Why should I care about such a thing? I looked at the crest of land below the graveyard, and imagined all the soil dropping away to show me the corpses therein. I had once tried to engage Susannah in discussion of Religion, but she was not very interested in the subject, or, at least, she was not interested in my thoughts on the subject. I was not very interested either, but had thought she would be, because I saw her in Church every Sunday.

'But you are always there, too,' said she. 'It does not signify anything, other than that we both adhere to the convention of attending Church.'

I'd felt a little saddened that she had not noticed I was occasionally daringly absent on Sundays. 'Perhaps,' I said, 'but, Miss Prendergast, I am not always present at Church.'

'Well, you may have the freedom to absent yourself, but I do not,' she said. 'I do as I am told to do.' She said this with a smile I could not quite interpret.

There on the forested Isle, the road wended down before us to a settlement far below.

'It is quiet to-day,' my Cannibal said.

Smoke came like tufts of wool from the tiny chimneys and, marking the northernmost border of the village, a black river slithered here and there out of the trees. A gull circled overhead, although there was no sea in sight. And everywhere—beyond the village and the fields, dominating every hill and slope, everywhere I could see—an impenetrable wilderness of silver-green leaves. Brave little settlement, huddled amidst indifferent Nature.

'You described these roads as treacherous, sir, but they seem quite tranquil,' I called ahead to my Cannibal. My voice cut sharply through the thin air. As I made my remark, however, I felt anew my sense of strangeness: that the black river below or the green wilderness stretching in every direction, just beyond the civilised town and fields, might hold any curiosity, or wonder, or horror.

'Treacherous is as treacherous does,' he told me over his shoulder, then paused to stretch his back. 'There has been many an attack along this way.'

I halted Tigris as she drew level with my Cannibal and looked out at the very image of the Pastoral Ideal. 'On this matter, you are better informed than I,' I said. 'Is it the Black Men? Shall we meet roving bands with spears?'

'No, it is not the Black Men,' said my Cannibal.

'No?'

'Your countrymen have been upon this Isle near forty years, now, Englishman,' he said.

'Indeed, I believe that is true.'

'Forty years!' he said, and gave me a look of deep Irishness.

Why was every damned—I do not care, damned be damned—conversation in that place like trying to see a figure through a window on a dark night in a storm, while blindfolded?

'Do you speak Irish, sir, as your native tongue?' I asked. I thought in a flash that perhaps his obtuseness might be explained by some imperfect translation.

'I speak it, yes, concurrently with English—that is, English is as native to me as Irish.'

I looked at the man's hairy face and made to investigate further his remarks, but was stymied rather by the delicious scent of roasting meat on the breeze.

'Oh, look at the sun! It is noon,' I said.

'I also speak French,' he told me.

'Oh—very good,' I said. In fact, I was in particular need of someone with French. Mamma made a remark to me in that language when we parted, and I had been unable decipher it myself. But when I tried to find the words to ask my Cannibal to translate for me, I found that I was quite suddenly upon the very brink of tears. I shook my head and put that matter away for another time, when I would not weep while asking.

'On to a more pressing matter—shall we rest, and eat, and warm ourselves in the village below? Or is it treacherous also?' I asked, and the weeping feeling melted away.

'You are not surprised that I speak French?'

'No, for the world is a large place, with many possibilities in it. I salute you—I am afraid I did not bother much with French.'

This seemed to satisfy him. 'I concur with your remark about the size of the world. It is large, that is true. As to your question,' he said, 'the village is friendly enough to travellers. Why should it not be? They bring money, and sometimes Wives. But we ought not stop. We won't reach the station by nightfall if we do.'

'Is there no inn where we might warm our bones, at least for a moment?' I heard the plaintive yearning in my own voice.

'Oh—aye, there is an inn,' he said, and set off once more.

'Is it a better place than that in which we met?' I asked, urging Tigris to go along with him, side by side.

'Who can measure such a thing?'

'Well, a man such as I, who has passed the night in a bed more akin to the Rack, after a supper most indifferent, can measure such a thing,' I said.

'You are accustomed to greater comforts than travelling on a cold day without rest, and sleeping on a bed akin to the Rack, and eating badly—and mixing with unsavoury sorts,' said he, with what I took to be a good dose of personal insight. 'Yet it will be a discomfort such as you have not yet experienced if we must pass the night in the Wilderness, without the proper gear, and are eaten alive, or else freeze. If you wish to stop at the inn, you must stop there, and pass the night, and set out again to-morrow. But I will not wait for you, and you must find the way yourself,' he told me. 'Why not simply press on with me, and save yourself the trouble, and the cost?'

'It is expensive, then?' I asked.

'No—quite cheap, in terms of money.'

The day stretched before me like a Wasteland of Starvation and Torture, and the breath of roasting meat on the breeze danced like a Siren's call to my nose.

'What is it that would eat us alive?'

'What say you now?'

'You told me we would be eaten alive in the Wilderness. What Creature would do such a thing?'

'Why, the tiger-wolf, for one,' said my Cannibal. 'And who knows what darker and subtler Beast slinks yet undiscovered amongst these trees?'

'You echo my own thoughts, sir, with your latter remark.' The man smiled. 'We are more and more in agreement.'

The forested slopes rose ever higher around us.

'It occurs to me that I do not know your name,' said I.

'Indeed not. Nor I yours,' said he, and left it at that, for a cart and horses driven by a woman with flame-red hair had rattled into view. Two red-haired children leant over the sides of the cart from amongst the covered baskets lashed therein, watching me with great sharp eyes.

'Good morning, madam,' I called, with an appropriate salute, as this party drew nearer.

''Tis afternoon,' she said, and gave me a look that indicated she had said too much, and urged her two horses on. Such speaking faces the people have here! If only I could understand the language of their expressions.

'Cautious matron,' said my Cannibal approvingly.

'Would you care to ride a little?'

'Perhaps when we are past the village.'

A black stallion stood silhouetted for a moment against the crest of the hill as we wound our way down. Is this the substance of Life? A series of images, some fine, some foul, most humdrum, interconnected so minutely and transitioning from one to the next with such smoothness one might blink and find oneself catapulted from a humble life as a third son in England and into the boots of some harpoon-clanking lunatic quite upside down in weird Barbary looking at a horse on a hill? And one a helpless visitor, as a person in an art gallery who has no appreciation for Painting?

The prismatic vagaries of thought are ever subject to the more secular matter of the Stomach, like the gross Anchor of an airy ship. My hopes for breakfast that morning had not been high, but were nevertheless disappointed. We had departed too early to be served, although I had paid in advance. I had had an apple, and plenty of water, but I made my approach of the village in the valley with hunger roaring through me like the tiger-wolf. I had been lulled by his easy companionship into forgetting my Cannibal's penchant for man-flesh, but my own longing for meat returned this thought to me. I stole a glance at the hairy head, picked out with eyes and a pink nose and a mouth which opened from within. There was within my breast the stirrings of sympathy for the desperation which might drive a man to eat another.

'I am a touch peckish,' I ventured, as the iron fist of starvation clenched my guts.

'Good kangaroo steamer awaits us tonight,' said my Cannibal. 'There is a woman at the station, Mary, who cooks well with what little she has.'

'I do not know what that is,' I said. 'Kangaroo steamer, you see.'

'Then warm yourself with the expectation of a pleasant surprise at journey's end.'

I gave a weary sigh. The man was as opaque as a brick wall. 'As we are sharing the road, sir, and have thrown our lots together, even for a short time,' I said, 'why do we not converse a little of ourselves, and see how Fate has so drawn us here?'

'Fate?' he said. 'I do not believe in it.'

'Ah, no—an expression, merely.'

'Indeed.'

'What, then, *do* you believe?'

'What a question! A large question for a small day.'

'How is the day small, sir?' asked I, looking about me at the generous land.

'It is small because it is quite ordinary.'

'Not to me, sir! I do not think I have passed an ordinary day since I departed England. Here I am, riding along upon balding "Tigris"—whose sire was a Lake—to a whaling-station!—to eat Steamed Kangaroo!—I ask you—'

'Man, you are raving.'

The Voice of Reason! That was rich, coming from the mouth of the man-eater.

He cast a smile into the heavens, or bared his teeth at them, anyhow. 'Ask me something, then, something I can answer, and I will tell you, and you will know me better.'

'What is kangaroo steamer?' I asked him.

'It is akin to jugged hare, but it is prepared with the flesh of the kangaroo. It makes a delectable repast.'

'Ah! Very well. I will make another question, as that one was not about you, and if the purpose is to better know you, I do not know you better for knowing about kangaroo steamer. Sir—have you a wife?'

'Yes, one or two.'

I suppose I do not truly believe that Bigamy is a sin worse than Cannibalism, but to my light-headed and unbreakfasted self, Cannibalism did seem the lesser evil. Do allow me to be clear: I am a Fool, perhaps, but not, medically speaking, an Idiot, and the more I discoursed with this unlikely Fellow, the better I perceived that he was a man of some wit and humanity, and perhaps was not the Vile Figure I had at first taken him to be. Nevertheless, evil is a scourge at all levels of Society, and his teeth, when the fur parted to show them, were exceedingly yellow.

'Do you know any women called Maryanne Maginn?' I asked him.

'Oh, I imagine so,' he said. 'Half a dozen, at the least.'

I paused. That was not useful. 'What is your . . . favourite food?' I asked.

'Nothing can surpass old Mary's kangaroo steamer, taken with bread and butter,' said he.

We had come to be somewhere: as we climbed a little rise in the generally downward road, we found a charming house set back from the thoroughfare. It was a wooden cottage with tidy hedgerows and a Goat tethered amongst flowers of some description, which therefore had mostly lost their heads. There was also a cabbage-patch evidently more loved than the flowers, for it was well enclosed against the Goat. The hearty redolence of roasting meat flooding from every window assaulted my senses and I drew Tigris to a halt.

'Not there,' said my Cannibal. 'Press on.'

I saw a feminine face peering at us from a window.

'Note the cabbages,' he added.

'Yes, I see,' I said.

'So it is certainly winter.'

'I see that, my friend.'

The woman at the window watched us as we departed.

'Comely face,' said my Cannibal.

'You may be correct, but I am unable to offer any comment on it. I know of only one comely face,' I said. When he did not ask me to elaborate upon this, I volunteered: 'I was to marry. Susannah is her name.'

He inclined his head but, again, did not press me for further detail.

Ah, Susannah Prendergast! I took out her miniature, in its little gold case, and looked upon her for a moment. Perhaps I did this rather ostentatiously, with a romantic sigh, to prompt my Cannibal to ask me about her. But he did not.

The Artist had not possessed any green paint, and so painted-Susannah's eyes were rather greyer than in reality, but aside from this, and the fact that no painting could accurately portray the Vividness of her glance, the delicate blue veins at her temples, and the little seashells of her ears, it was her exactly. Indeed, it was amazing how like her it was, given that I had been compelled to pay the (Catholic) Artist to attend our (heathenish) Church of England to make some discreet sketches in the pews. For I should not have suffered the embarrassment well of asking her to sit, and being denied.

Where did my thoughts take me when I beheld Susannah's likeness? The little picture was eloquent upon the subject of beauty, and all the good things tacitly understood to accompany beauty, whatever they were—honesty, perhaps, and charm, and wit, and other such things, I supposed. And Susannah herself? I thought of her as I had first seen her, in a pink dress with little golden flowers to match her hair, engulfed by the white-and-gold divan, when Mrs Prendergast had brought her to be introduced. There had been a frailty to her as she looked around at us. She had not said much, which, I suppose, was moderately correct of a girl so young. Still, she had not done well on that occasion, I am afraid. I was only glad Father was absent. She had worn quite a sorrowful expression upon her face, until Mrs Prendergast twitched her eyebrows perhaps one-tenth of an inch in a certain subtle way. At this signal, Susannah had started a little, and changed her expression, smiling, and looking wildly about the room for something upon which she might rest her glassy eyes. They fell upon the Chinoiserie cabinet and there stayed, and so she smiled desperately at this cabinet for some duration of time, wrenching her gaze away with visible difficulty when Mamma addressed her directly. Poor girl! Mamma had been kind.

Later, Mamma had spoken of her with a view to my middle brother John, but it was decided he could certainly do better, even if she came with money.

I thought of Susannah as I had last beheld her, looking grave in a subdued gown, almost as if she were in mourning. She was quiet on that occasion, too, but was in much greater possession of herself—perfect possession—saying little but a courteous farewell.

I do not mean to suggest that she never spoke; she spoke a great deal between those two times. Those two images I have of her, the first and last I had seen of her, I suppose do nothing to represent the person herself. Sometimes I had wished I could see through her white forehead and into her brain. If only I could read her thoughts, unfiltered by the many layers of politeness and convention through which we communicated! Sometimes she would sit with her hands clasped tightly together and listen to me with an air of impatience, as though she were eager to disagree. She had had a greater range of experience in life than my own, despite being a little younger—only now was I advancing upon her in that regard. Her mother was dead, and her father was in Burma, we were told, and he had tried to keep Susannah there, and found it most unsuitable, and thus she was sent to make her life with her great-grandmother in Norfolk.

A million worlds away, my Cannibal and I crested the rise, and there before us was the village. This place had the hastily erected air about it many such habitations do in the colonies, like a stage-set, and yet there were people going hither and thither with the same easy purpose just as they might in my own ancient village at Home.

The houses varied to a degree in size and profusion of chimneys, but all were stone or brick, and neatly kept on good, large plots of land. Indeed, they were oddly spaced one from the next, if one were to compare with an English village. It was much as if the inhabitants of the houses were feuding with their neighbours, and distanced themselves accordingly.

It seemed less cold amongst these signs of civilisation. After our long morning, it was a comfort to exchange quite ordinary nods with quite ordinary-looking country folk, although the wood smoke made my eyes smart, and there was one less-ordinary-looking countrywoman with a jaw like a brick and a bosom like a man-o'-war whose fierce aspect rather made me wish to retreat all the way back through the colony and across the seas to my childhood bed in Norfolk. The great, green hills swept upwards all around us, and the broad river glinted ahead. Upon one hill nestled a white church, and on another a brown.

The houses gave way to the Establishments of the village, which were larger and more plentiful than I might have expected: there was a General Store and Post Office, and a Dispensing Chemist's, a Bakery, a Butcher's, a Draper and Haberdasher's, a Saddlery, and a Bank. All were free-standing, with large, glass-paned windows, and oil lamps above these windows to illuminate the displays at night. The culmination of all these fine institutions was the Hotel. It was called the Royal, which was, let us say, an exaggeration. Nevertheless, it had a sufficiently pleasant aspect, and I cast yearning eyes towards it.

The Bank had given me pause. My first thought was that I ought to go within and withdraw some money against my letter of credit. My second thought was of my Cannibal's preoccupation with the treachery of the road. Weighing the matter, I decided I had best make do with the few coins I had about me, and wait until my return to the relatively more civilised Hobart-town. There, at least, I might take a room in a more habitable Establishment than the sink-hole of the previous night, which might have a safe, or, at least, a door with a functioning lock.

My Cannibal hailed an old man resting himself on a bench outside the General Store and Post Office, and they exchanged some words too rapid and particular for me to discern. A boy driving a sheep came along the road, and he either did not see me or did not care to see me, for I was obliged to move Tigris from his path. A surpassingly pretty girl with fair hair emerged from the Draper and Haberdasher's with a parcel clutched in her hands. I tried smiling at this individual; she did not look at me. Two plump matrons with various infants about their persons were engaged in serious Discourse outside the Chemist's. As I rode by, I heard one say to the other: 'There is nothing so good as soap and water, and old-fashioned elbow grease—and no Concoction will convince me otherwise.' A very small hand waved in regal fashion to me from somewhere within its mother's dress, and big eyes under fairy-down hair looked out. 'What is more,' the woman went on, 'I do not trust his expensive prescriptions, when everybody knows all a sick baby needs is a little bread soaked in wine, and some sago.' Her friend was nodding and grimacing in profound agreement. In all, this was a village with Life and Liveliness about it.

As I paraded along the thoroughfare upon my black steed, I found that the Royal Hotel was apparently Magnetised, for it was drawing me in by the stirrups.

Even in the face of my man-eating hunger, I paused for a moment to gaze beyond the Hotel at that silent river. I could see the broad and drifting surface troubled with reflected trees, clouds, and the stone arches of the bridge. The water was dark, like tea, but not tea, or whisky, or watered-down ink—but it had the air of freshness about it, and it glimmered like something that had lived many millions of years ago, and now had distilled into something rare.

'You advised me of your hunger,' said my Cannibal, who, I saw, had paused, and stood regarding me. 'And I advised you of our need to press on. I shall leave you to choose your own action next, as you, like me, are one of the Free, and may do as you wish.' And he strode away, towards the bridge, without further ado or farewell.

Perhaps public houses are the secret of Life. I know the map of my own life can be signposted by public houses.

There were two mounts tethered already at the trough by the steps, a very fine grey stallion, and a dear little grey pony. A boy lounged against the bottom step. Now there is a Law of Nature worth investigation!—the ubiquity of a particularity of child who, by virtue of some no doubt Scientifically measurable confluence of poverty, dimples, freckles, impudence, wit, selfishness and charm, can only be called an Urchin. I must make a note.

The Urchin in question said, 'Leave her here, sir. I shall watch her.'

'Thank you, my lad,' I told him, and, dismounting, gave him a penny from my pouch.

I saw my Cannibal looking back at me from the middle of the bridge. He raised a hand in wry salute and I, proudly, hailed him in return. He was correct; I was one of the Free, and would do as I wished, and I wished to take a good meal and pass a comfortable night before going forth to find the floating Platform or whatever the whaling-station might in fact be.

'Penny don't buy much these days,' the Urchin said. 'Economy as it is.' He gave a manly shake of the head. 'Wool price down, sir. Read in the *Colonial Times*.'

Mark: the land where Urchins read the news-paper for tidings of the Economy like the soberest of chaps!

'I shall give you another when I return,' I said.

'Fanks.'

Tigris made no objection to my tethering her to the post; she immediately occupied herself by drinking the water in the trough.

'What happened to her?'

'What do you mean?'

'She's all patchy, sir. All patchy.'

'Well, never mind that,' I said. 'I am so hungry I feel quite faint.' Urchins respond to nice, brisk candour from their betters.

'Go and have a bite to eat then, sir. Not the rabbit pie,' he added. 'It ain't rabbit.'

'Oh—thank you.'

"Nother penny, sir,' he said. 'Advice don't come cheap neither.'

'I shall give you your balance when I emerge, and it shall be dependent on the usefulness of your advice, and the safety of my horse,' I told the little lad. 'I have counted the bald patches; there are seven, and I do not wish to come out and find more.' Now that was a silly remark. What was I suggesting? That the boy would pluck hairs from Tigris while I was indoors?

I mounted the steps quickly, to escape my embarrassment, then immediately returned, and removed my harpoons from where I had lashed them, and again climbed to the door, harpoons over my shoulder.

And there was a homely place! An image of the Gaol of a Hotel I had passed the previous night in, with my Prison Cell of a room, and Torture Device of a bed, went before me. With this array of horrors in my mind, I might better enjoy the comforts of the Royal, by contrast. Royal it was not, indeed, but there were honestly worn carpets upon the floorboards, and large windows pouring honeyed sun—where they had contrived to find honeyed sun on such a clear cold day, I did not know—into the tap-room, and a fire crackling merrily in the great hearth. The room was taken up with two convivially long wooden tables running almost from the far wall to the bar. Surely the village entire could be seated at such mighty boards, although that afternoon they were unpeopled but for one dishevelled man propping his elbow by his glass.

A woman of indefinable age—the sort who might be thirty-five or fifty-three—leant upon the bar, stout and red, as a proprietress ought to be. Beside her was an aged farming-type with a pipe poking out from amidst his respectable grey beard. The proprietress was making some concession to work, with a rag bunched in her hand, but was waxing lyrical, gesturing with the rag in the air to punctuate the following remark: 'And I recalled, 'twas not the twill, but the tweed!' This induced a great shout of laughter in the farmer. He removed his pipe in order to make the exclamation of mirth, and then soberly replaced it.

'Oh, good afternoon!' the proprietress called to me. 'Come in, sir. Warm yourself. It is cold—I was only just outside myself. This morning's frost still has not cleared.' I had the sensation once again that the entire village was the set for a play, and these two had been posed and ready to begin a rehearsed show upon my entrance.

There was a velvety old armchair by the hearth, soft with a thousand pairs of buttocks, a relic older than the colony itself. I dropped myself there and rested just as my Cannibal had been when I first beheld him. It was true I felt a sense of unreality, but the chair's threadbare upholstery had subsumed the heat of the fire, which transferred back into me, and that was real.

I felt a suffusion of nostalgic comfort so strongly it made me a little sad with the general longings of lost childhood one feels in such moments, especially as the proprietress had spoken in the unmistakable accent of Cornwall, whence had come my childhood nurse, as well.

Nurse had been amazingly unable to peel an apple with any delicacy, and from a robust red apple she would present us with a few poor porcelain-thin slivers of apple-flesh to eat. I remember my own mother taking the paring knife and the apple from Nurse's hands one picnic, upon witnessing the destruction and travesty of Nurse's attempt, and peeling the apple herself, the skin dropping in one great curl in her lap. There was then a game with the apple peel, in which the peel was dropped in a certain way, to fall into the initials of my future love. It was all Cs and Os, as one might not need a Mystical Nature to divine apple peel might naturally fall, although that was significant for Freddie, because of Charlotte Oxford.

'What is it you shall be taking, sir?' the proprietress asked me, abandoning her old friend to come and loom benignly. She wore her brown shawl crossed over her bosom and her hair in a discreet cap, like any good country-woman at Home.

'Have you kangaroo steamer?' I asked.

'No, sir. I am sorry, but I do not touch kangaroo-flesh. I was compelled, when first I came here, to eat more of it than I should ever have cared to. We do have rabbit pie, which is especially hearty to-day, white bread and cheese, bacon, cutlets, pork twice-laid, rum, gin and ale—and cider aplenty.'

She went on to list some other comestibles, but I struggled to pay her any attention, so great was my hunger and so deep my weariness.

So lulled was I by the warmth of the room and of the welcome, and the 'especial heartiness', that I asked for rabbit pie and cider, despite the Urchin's word of caution.

As if to confirm the goodness of the place, the old farmer puffed a smoke ring directly over his bald head and sat gazing beneficently at me with the ring floating above him like nothing so much as a halo. The other man, the down-at-heels man who was seated alone at one of the tables, took a final swig of his dregs, then rose and left.

'Where are you going, Beasley?' the farmer called after him, but there was no response. At least, there was none that I heard, as I leant back and drifted almost instantly into a dream in which I plunged through a sea of rustling leaves and saw a circle of pained white faces looking everywhere but at my mother.

I HAD ALREADY BEEN FORGOTTEN

THE PROPRIETRESS TOLD ME SHE did not wish to wake me, and thus woke me. With a hearty and humorous kind of servility, she brought me to sit at the bar to eat, placing me a polite stool or two away from the farmer.

A pair of neatly dressed girl-children came into the Hotel with a pot to be filled with beer for their father. They were very similar in looks, although one was taller, and the other had a livid purple birthmark on her face. The proprietress tended to them, and sent them off, saying sternly, 'You tell that man to make it last, for I do not wish to sell him more to-day,' which seemed rather counter to sound business practices.

All the while I devoured the pie she had brought me with a relish probably disproportionate to its simplicity. I thought of the Urchin's warning against this fine pie, and scoffed, and resolved he should not have another penny for his bad advice.

The proprietress and the farmer had evidently consulted quietly together as I slept, for next they put to me their guess as to my Purpose in their valley. They told me that I was a farmer myself, seeking a parcel of land to buy, and that although I spoke rather better than a humble farmer (they said), all men were equal here, except for those who were not. I was a gentleman farmer, they told me. Well! I was in luck, for it happened that they knew of a family with an established wheat farm which they wished to sell (at a fair price) in order to move north to be nearer their kin in Victoria, and were mostly not criminals (the local family or the northern kin or all involved, I was not sure). The farmhouse was without rival in the valley, and had a staircase imported from Italy, which was greatly admired by all who saw it. And Gentlemen Do Love Bread. This last said with some meaning.

'Everybody is selling something, here,' I said.

'The Economy is taking a downward turn,' the farmer said. 'I sold my sheep two, three year ago. Got in early.'

'Mr Green read the Economy in the clouds,' said the lady-publican. 'Now he is very comfortably Retired—if you do not mind my saying so, Mr Green,' she added, as an aside.

'I do not mind you saying what is true, Mrs Nancarrow.'

'Perhaps the sorry state of the Economy is why I cannot sell my harpoons,' said I.

'Yes, we did pass a few moments in trying to guess why you carried those,' she said. 'They do not speak to you being a farmer, although the look of you does.' She and the old man exchanged a glance rich with meaning.

'There is little future in whaling here, my lad,' Mr Green told me, leaning closer.

'Indeed. We have heard the whales are either dying in excessive numbers, and not replenishing themselves, or, at least, are no longer presenting themselves to be hunted,' said Mrs Nancarrow. 'Foolish creatures.'

''Tis a great pity,' said Mr Green. 'It was a mighty trade.'

'You see how the Economy is beset from all sides,' said Mrs Nancarrow to me.

'Wheat, oats and barley, and apples, in the south,' said Mr Green, and I saw again the skill of my mother's hands as she peeled the red fruit. 'And cattle, perhaps. That is the future.'

'And timber, besides!' said Mrs Nancarrow.

'That is true. Timber is also the future.'

Here was a necessary pause in our conversation, for two red-coated soldiers threw open the door and stood surveying the room in the imperious way particular to coarse young men in smart uniforms. They were large men, broad-chested and daunting, especially in the rifle-guns slung over their shoulders. I sat very still, but the woman served them gamely; they ordered beer, and drank it with accomplished speed, while Mrs Nancarrow chatted to them about the State of the Judiciary System, on which topic they held no opinions. They departed, wiping their mouths.

As if there had been no interruption, the old farmer observed, 'Wheat farmer has no need of harpooning, in general.'

'Well, as to your guess,' I said, 'you are partly right. My father is a farmer, and my eldest brother will inherit it—the farm—when he—my father—dies. I am quite free of the obligation of farming, being the third son, which suits me well, as I did not take naturally to it. That is the extent of it. I do not wish to buy any land, I am afraid, nor wheat. I am going north-east to a whaling-station—which I also do not wish to buy—to perhaps at last divest myself profitably of these harpoons.'

'It seems an awful lot of trouble for what may be little reward,' said Mrs Nancarrow. 'Although I do admit I do not know anything of the price of harpoons—or irons, as I believe they are sometimes called.'

'An awful lot of trouble, Mrs Nancarrow, you are right,' said the farmer, Mr Green.

'I do not suppose you are acquainted with any whalers?' I asked them, with the presupposition that they might help me find a buyer and save me the onward journey.

Mrs Nancarrow laughed. 'No! No. Not acquainted. We have the odd seafaring sort through here, on his way north, or south, but no, my dear sir—we do not know any whalers here in the fields. And—you say you did not take to farming, but neither are you a whaler. That is clear to me, even with your harpoons.'

'You are entirely right in that, madam. And it is true, the harpoons are incidental to my true Purpose here. I am looking for a woman.'

'Yes, that is a difficulty still, although I hear the Government is taking measures. There are ten men to every woman here, and fifty to every honest one.'

'No honest men, though,' said Mr Green.

'Yes, that is true,' said Mrs Nancarrow. 'It is only fair of you to make that observation.'

'No, madam, forgive me. I am looking for a particular woman, some years my elder, I believe, and not for the purpose of . . . matrimony. She is the Relative of an elderly lady I know, Mrs Prendergast, who is herself a Relative of a young lady who is very dear to me—although there is no relation between the young lady and the woman I seek, for they are from different branches of the elderly lady's family—and the elderly lady has given me some money to cover my expenses, and it has been intimated to me that, if I am successful, and return successfully, then perhaps I may hope to be nearly worthy of the young lady's hand, or at least slightly less unworthy—'

'Stop! Sir, you are quite confused.'

I did not know if there was anything much that passed for gentle society in Van Diemen's Land, although I supposed the Lieutenant-Governor and Lady Franklin must have had *someone* to talk to. Perhaps it was only that it was so new for me to be solitary, without even a servant, and to be mixing with people so very different from me, but I felt refreshed by the naturalness and frankness with which people spoke to one another. The society—rather, Society—I was accustomed to is a discreet Mechanism, and the difference between a pair of white shoulders angled ever-so-slightly towards one and ever-so-slightly away from one can spell triumph, or ruin. Not so in that place!

I had become quite red: I could feel it in my cheeks. 'Yes. Do forgive me. That is too much. Allow me to put it plainly. On behalf of her Relative, I am looking for a woman called Maryanne Maginn, who was transported here as a young girl some thirty years ago or more, from England.'

'From England? She has not an English name.'

'I believe she had some family connexion to Ireland.'

'And transported thirty years ago. How old would she be now?'

'Oh, in her middle forties.'

'So she was young indeed when she was transported. I do not think they ought to transport any soul, boy or girl, below the age of twenty-one,' Mrs Nancarrow said. 'It is not right. They are too unformed to endure the hardships of the sentence and emerge bettered, or, at least, not broken.'

'Wrongdoing is wrongdoing, and better to be sent here than to be hanged,' said Mr Green. 'Or would you have them hang more children in England?'

'I would not, no,' said Mrs Nancarrow, and was quiet for a moment, but was evidently unable to present a solution to the problem of the injustices of the transportation system. 'I wonder how many Maryanne Maginns there are in Christendom?' she said.

'But are we in Christendom?' mused the farmer.

'I should say! Have we got churches or haven't we?' Mrs Nancarrow said, and, 'I cannot say I have heard the name precisely, but it sounds just such a name as any number of girls might have. There is Maryanne O'Connell, the midwife. How old is she, would you say?' she asked Mr Green.

'I shouldn't like to guess,' said he. 'I have a granddaughter called Maryanne,' he added, to me. 'But she is six, and was never a Convict, so that is no help to you, sir.'

'Perhaps you might try the Police Magistrate's office, down in Hobarton. But how you will get an introduction, I do not know. Or—where do they keep records?' she asked Mr Green.

He intimated with his shoulders that he also was not in possession of that knowledge. 'Record house?' he suggested.

'Well, I do not know. Meanwhile, there is a drop of rain,' Mrs Nancarrow said, and indeed, there was the peppering of raindrops against the glass, and the shadows of the drops speckling the floor. 'Will you be going on this afternoon, sir, or stopping here to-night?'

'Rain will set in,' said the farmer. 'The clouds this morn.'

The farmer had a little of my Cannibal's opacity about him. I had forgotten my Cannibal until that moment, and the thought of him walking north, with his hairy face, alone and in the rain, made me miss him rather.

'I believe I will be pressing on, madam. Although your Establishment is homely—in the best sense—I have a wish to find my companion.'

'The road is quite treacherous, you know, sir, and it is perhaps unwise to continue to-day. We have charming bed-rooms furnished with every necessity. Many have a prospect of the river which brings peace to the very Mind. Why do you not stop here to-night, and make a good start to-morrow morning, with plenty of daylight ahead of you, and finer weather (I imagine—Mr Green can tell you for certain, if he will be so good as to cast a glance at the sky), and perhaps company, if Bobbin and Clark are riding north to the labouring for McNamara as they told me they might?'

'Are they whalers, madam?' I asked.

'Oh no, they are men. I mean farmhands. Mr McNamara runs cattle some way past your whaling-station.'

This information did not move me. 'You are exceedingly kind to think of my safety, madam, and for that I thank you. But I am resolved. Let me make payment, and thank you again, and be on my way,' I said, standing.

Mrs Nancarrow and the farmer exchanged an inscrutable look.

Mr Green obligingly gazed out of the window, and said, 'The rain will worsen to-night, and grow finer on the morrow, although there may be a little cloud to the south.'

'Will the rain become heavy enough to flood the road?' asked Mrs Nancarrow. 'For the road does flood, you know!' she added to me.

'No, not quite so heavy as that,' said the farmer. 'But heavy enough.'

I have always been fond of rain, and bad weather, although I confess I like it rather better when I am warmly indoors, and it is out. I shall never forget the afternoon I rushed Susannah Prendergast and my cousin Charlotte Oxford into the little white summerhouse by the lake as gigantic drops of rain pelted us from a clear sky. We stood beneath the stone portico, gazing up at the storm roiling towards us from behind the hills, the black clouds eating into the blue. Charlotte and Susannah had been gathering violets, and they had made garlands for their hair, that regal purple against the golden head and the dark.

Charlotte said, 'If you are to stand with us, it is necessary to wear a flower in your hair.' And she pulled a damp and wilted bloom from her head and tucked it behind my ear. It was sisterly; the understanding was that she would marry Freddie.

Susannah said, 'When shall we three meet again? In thunder, lightning, or in rain?'

I had thought this a pretty line of verse, and had discovered later, from Mamma, that it was Shakespeare, and therefore I had carefully read the play in question, and came away quite horrified.

Now, I said, 'I am a farmer's son, as I have said. I am not afraid of a little rain. The weather, at least, in this England of the Pacific, does agree with me, however strange it is here in other ways.'

Mrs Nancarrow said, 'Well, I do not wish to be Mrs I-told-you-so, and therefore I wish you a safe journey.'

'Thank you, madam.' I paid her the price she named, which seemed on the expensive side of fair—ah, the Economy!—and I gave her a coin or two more, which she told me she could not possibly take, while stowing them in her apron pocket.

'Where did Beasley go?' she asked Mr Green, as a by-the-way.

The farmer said, 'He went off, is all I could observe.'

'A-horse, are you?' asked Mrs Nancarrow.

'Yes, I have a good horse. Good enough. Well, she will do.'

'Very well, sir. You are a man grown, and I have done my duty,' she announced, and took my dish and empty glass, and sallied away behind the bar. Mr Green returned his attention to his own glass. I tipped my hat to the room at large, but I had already been forgotten.

Perhaps I am an honest Vandemonian

A DEEP COLD ROSE FROM the river's unhurried surface, flooding me, as it were, with sensation from a place that truly was Elsewhere. What huge and sinuous bodies might live out their life-spans at the bottom of that dark river, untroubled by man or tiger-wolf? I fancied my eyes were harpoons and shot them fathoms below my feet to a great water-snake with scales like drifting lace.

    A dark-haired woman mounted side-saddle upon a pony meandered towards the village, idly dragging her switch against the low stone wall of the bridge. She was bare-headed, but wrapped well about the shoulders against the cold. A dull and unrhythmic thudding sounded in the air around us. I looked at her with the resigned acceptance of one locked in a strange dream.

'How deep is it?' I asked her.

'Oh, deep enough that you would drown if you cannot swim,' she said, from within a dream of her own. 'But not so much deeper than that. Why do you ask me?'

'I was imagining to myself what queer creatures might live within.'

'Well, there are minnows,' she said, gently.

The little pony carried her away. The thudding continued in her absence, and the bridge trembled.

I felt some urgency in finding my Cannibal, and yet I found myself rather transfixed by the river. The rain had stopped as I left the Royal, and now it began again. Little glassy rounds sprinkled the river's surface. Tiny black fish with eyes like pricks of light pirouetted in long columns across my mind's eye.

'You told me there were seven bald patches on her, sir,' the little Urchin had said when I re-emerged from the hotel. 'But you see there are nine. You did not see behind her ears, I fink. Two pennies is the balance.'

Now that the Urchin had showed them to me, I wondered how I had missed the half-moons of bald skin behind her ears. I imagined nine bald patches dripping from Tigris just as the boot polish had, and dropping into the water, and swimming away, and leaving me mounted upon a perfect black horse.

The wish for a little boat arose in me, that I might set it upon the water and drift in it gently out to sea, or to whatever place this river would deliver me. I let Tigris move where she would, loosened my hold upon the reins, and slipped my feet from the stirrups. Further compounding my desire to rather abandon solid Earth and float away was the terrible sight upon the road ahead of me and the source of the thudding. This I had seen, but pretended I had not seen, lest I accidentally meet somebody's eyes: a dozen men, dressed in the felt brown-and-yellow of the Unfree, chained one to the next at the ankle and digging in motley disorder by the road on the opposite bank. The red-coated soldiers from the Royal leant upon their weapons in rather an uninspiring manner and watched. Another man patrolled the line—indeterminately Free or Unfree, as he was dressed in neither Soldier nor Convict attire. He was, at least, clearly a finer class of person than the unfortunates in the Chain-Gang, for he wielded the twin distinctions of the whip and unfettered ankles. This individual shouted such encouragements as You Fucking Dogs Dig Faster This Road Will Flood and Honest People Must Travel It—I merely report. The words skimmed across the black satin of the water, rebounded in my ears and had the effect of putting my feet back in the stirrups. The dark-haired woman had passed this scene unperturbed and unmolested, and I must do the same.

The grimaces of the thralls were pitiful to see. The bored attitudes of the soldiers were somehow as melancholy. They gave no indication that they recognised me from the Royal, nor indeed that they saw me at all.

One of the chained men had been lashed very recently. Dark stripes of blood had seeped through the felt of his back.

Tigris and I went by with our heads down, the steady thud of pickaxes trembling the ground.

'Afternoon,' the supervisor called to me, with an insouciant glance.

'Good afternoon, sir,' said I.

'Enjoying the vista?'

'Ah—yes, it is a fine . . . vista.'

'And that big-titted piece on the pony as went by. Bouncing merrily along.'

I ignored this coarse remark.

'What did you say together? I saw you talking.'

'We talked briefly of the river. I asked her how deep it was, and she told me it was deep enough to drown in.'

'All water is deep enough to drown in,' said the man. 'That is the nature of water.'

'I do not know much about the nature of water.'

'Well. You cannot disagree with me.'

I could! But I did not.

'Fine enough day for it,' he added, grinning, as the rain pattered upon the brim of my hat.

'I suppose it could be worse,' I said.

The moment came when I had to choose to halt Tigris, or allow her to walk me away from the scene, and, with an unreasonable pang of politeness, I stopped.

'Sorry lot, ain't they?' The man surveyed the men of the Chain-Gang with a proprietorial air and cracked his whip against the ground. Tigris had neither the spirit nor the brains to shy away.

'There but for the Grace of God go we,' I said.

'Certainly, if by the Grace of God you rape or murder, or attempt escape from Her Majesty's good justice,' he said. 'And where are you off to?'

'I am a simple Farmer's Son, travelling north,' I said, for I did not wish to give too much away to this disgusting fellow.

'Simple Farmer's Son, my arse.'

'How dare you,' I said, agog at my own daring.

He laughed.

'Shut your fucking gob, Biggins,' said one of the soldiers, with an air of some affection—and thus our niceties ended. This Discourse had not bettered me, nor informed, nor entertained, nor united me in sympathy to my fellow man, these being the four purposes of talk amongst people, according to *Dainty Conversation for the Drawing-Room: a Guide for Young Ladies and Gentlemen*. This was a book my mother had given me some years previously, before she was gently detained in the attic for her own good, and I wished I had had it to give the man with the whip. I imagined him reading it by candlelight in some mean accommodation, taking notes on the backs of the salacious drawings that circulate amongst such men, and practising his pleasantries upon the Convicts. Why, Horsham, might I compliment you upon your pornographic Tattoo? It should make a striking Lamp-shade, after you are hanged.

If you wish, I might refer you to a good Tanner I know—or perhaps I will refer your Executioner.

There was some undercurrent of meaning in that place that I was unable to fathom. There seemed a mode of being that everybody, perhaps from so high as the Lieutenant-Governor to so low as the lowliest thrall, understood. Everybody but I! I had the notion that my Cannibal might be the Bridge between my reasonable, English self, and the unplumbed depths of uncanniness of the local people, hidden behind the thin and unconvincing face of Normality. Or was he a bridge *over* the unplumbed depths? I supposed that was more logical. But a bridge to where?

I reckoned I had passed perhaps two hours in the Royal. Therefore, if I urged Tigris into a faster gait than my Cannibal could walk, I would necessarily meet him in less than that time. My Cannibal had said we would reach the station that day, and therefore I would find him some time before the station, while it was light (as I judged the sun would set in a few hours), and we would proceed onwards together to our destination. Was that how time and distance worked? And did they work in the same way here as at Home? It seemed correct, but I had not done well at such problems at school, and I did not know if Newton's Laws applied in quite the same way in the Antipodes. And was this all the domain of Mr Newton, in any case? He had to do with prisms, hadn't he? Perhaps I was attributing to him a greater field of knowledge than he had truly commanded because he was the only Scientist whose name I could remember.

Nevertheless, I called to mind the clear arc of my apple core that morning, from my hand to the ground, and the amused common-sense of my Cannibal, and felt assured that things would be well.

It took Tigris more than one attempt to discover a trot, and then a canter, but once comfortably settled in that stride, we made good time. The road was wide and quite well-kept, following the river as it wended northwards. The trees on either side grew deeper, and the last few holdings fell away, and the cold became keener, and the rain fell harder. The sun sank, as it ought, towards the Western Horizon, and the shadows reached out across the road to nip at Tigris's heels.

Following some idle train of thought, my mind turned to the woman on the pony who had spoken to me about the river. What colour were her eyes? I had a picture of her face in my mind: her eyes were green, but not like Susannah's, which sparkled with merriment. The woman's eyes were a serious, dark green that did not provoke laughter, but only calm. (And the bosom! Like enormous blancmanges!—guiltily, guiltily I thought of burying my face in it, and other such embraces. Do better, man! Think instead of her kind voice, and her natural manner! And yet a woman's body contorted before my eyes.)

There was a growing pain in my belly I had tried to ignore, but which had grown more and more persistent as

I travelled. I became hot, and perspiration sprouted from my forehead. I went on confusedly, lost alternately in thoughts of the river-woman and a sorrowful fixation upon the gymnastic rabbit pie in my belly. I remembered the Urchin at the Royal once more and resolved to pay him the penny I owed him for his advice regarding the rabbit pie on my return journey. I thought that I really ought to take Urchins more seriously. No doubt they were worldlier than I.

It was on a long and sheltered stretch of road that I found myself compelled to halt Tigris with some urgency. She was too clod-headed to immediately obey my command, and so I half climbed, half tumbled from her as she wandered to a lazy stop. Sweating in hideous profusion, I catapulted the rabbit pie from me in two unspeakable ways. There was I, base human, in foul torment amongst the trees, as little jewelled birds hopped merrily beneath overhanging branches. Wiping my poor face with my handkerchief, which I looked at, then dropped in disgust, I staggered some little way farther into the trees, and undressed to sacrifice my undershirt for a viler Purpose I shall not here describe. Oh, shameful secret! My hands trembled so I could hardly button my shirt once again. The earth was hard, and I could not bury the undershirt, and so I folded it as neatly as I was able and left it by the discarded handkerchief as I wavered my feeble way back to Tigris. She was plucking with rubbery lips at a bush and demonstrating very little sensitivity to my bodily horrors.

My mother would not have approved of my leaving my soiled things there. Indeed, I did not approve of it either, but I felt so weak, and wished only to be gone. The rain will wash them, I said to myself, and someone will find them, and I wish that person well of them. Thus did I justify leaving such disgusting items for another to find.

I had no sooner pulled myself back into the saddle gone dark with rainwater than I espied a man on horseback waiting right ahead of me, quite in the middle of the road. I had been so downcast I had not seen him at all until I had the advantage of Tigris's height. My first feeling was embarrassment, and a hope that he had not heard the horrible experience of the dual expulsion of bad not-rabbit from my guts. Was this my Cannibal, who had somehow acquired a horse? I should be ashamed if it were he. But I could see the man was not hairy enough. Indeed, though his face was shadowed, in fact it was Beasley, the rough man from the Royal, atop the fine grey horse I had seen tethered there. I urged Tigris to a walk and tried to turn her back the way we had come. Beasley slid a hand inside his coat. I wiped my damp brow with my coat sleeve and cast a longing look at my filthy handkerchief, which I could just see through the trees.

'Halt, man! I do not wish you any harm,' Beasley called. 'Only come here and let us talk.'

I urged Tigris on, away, but the stupid Creature made the unwise choice to sidle to the roadside to nip at the bush once more. I did, with some tugging, eventually convince her to go forwards, but Beasley had had all the time he required to come at quite a leisurely pace close enough that I could count his eyebrow hairs. All I could think of at that moment was—my God, he is an ugly man! He had a great, jutting brow, topped with a single eyebrow creeping from ear to ear. His chin was identical to his forehead, only upside down, and his beard a thick hairy line, like the eyebrow, so the effect was of a man with his face half underwater, and reflected back up at him. This ghoulish Creature kept one hand loosely upon the reins, and the other inside his coat.

'You are ill,' he said.

'Any man might become ill,' said I, proudly.

'It is dysentery.'

'It is rabbit pie.'

'Ah!—from the Royal. So much the worse,' he said, smiling. 'The woman does not use rabbit, you know. Still, I'm glad to hear you don't carry a contagion.'

'Is dysentery a contagion?' I asked.

'Is it not? When one man falls ill with it, his fellows fall ill with him. Therefore, it is a contagion.'

'Unless it is caused by some influence they all share in common, like bad water, which is what I am led to understand is the case.'

'Perhaps you are led to understand wrongly. Scientific Discourse aside, if it is not dysentery, then I shall not become ill from your things, and so I am glad.'

'You should not become ill from them, anyway, for you have no cause to be near them,' I said. 'Who are you to speak to me?'

'In fact, who are you?'

'A traveller,' I said. 'An honest Englishman. Can you say the same?'

'Why should I wish to?' he asked, and then said, 'Oblige me.'

'How do you expect I might oblige?' I asked.

'Well, I put it incorrectly. Actually, it is I who will oblige you. Do you know,' he said, with a conversational air, 'your horse is stolen?'

'No—no, she is not!' I said. 'I bought her this morning—indeed—there are Witnesses to this.'

'Oh, I am sure there are,' he said. 'It was a German fellow, was it, who sold it to you?'

'Yes, he was German . . .'

Beasley gave a great shout of laughter. 'That is my dear Engel. He is a thief—or, well, not a thief, but deals with thieves. He is a dealer of stolen horse-flesh. Very well-known as such. I suppose you bought her hastily, in some dark alley?'

I felt the slow creep of dread sucking away the urgency of my fear, leaving something insidious worming about within me. 'Even if you are correct, sir,' said I, 'and I have made a mistake, it is an innocent one, and no just Law would incriminate me.'

'I sincerely do not know how you could be in this place and yet believe the Law has any aroma of Justice about it.'

Indeed, the lingering horror of the Chain-Gang I had witnessed upon that very road was with me still.

'If I bought the horse fairly, and in good faith, and without knowledge she might be stolen, and if I surrender her to the authorities if asked, how can I be accused of any wrongdoing?'

'Well, you know now the beast is stolen, and yet you ride it. Is that not wrongdoing?'

'Forgive me, sir, but I have only your word for it that she is stolen,' I said.

'Why should I lie?'

'You told me yourself you had no desire to call yourself an honest Englishman.'

'Perhaps I am an honest Vandemonian.'

'I have been given to understand there is no such thing.'

Beasley laughed once more. 'You and your understanding of things!'

'In any case,' I said, 'this trouble is mine, and has nothing to do with you.' I thought once more of the river-woman's deep green eyes and was bolstered by the memory of their sweet calm. 'Permit me to go on.'

'Oh! I shall, by and by,' said Beasley. 'This trouble of yours, as you acknowledge it is, is easily resolved, to the benefit of both. Let us come to an arrangement, like civilised men. You are in grave peril, sir, of Arrest and Confinement, if you are caught with such expensive stolen goods. And once you are arrested here—why, the road forks, and you are as likely to descend to degradation, Cannibalism and the gallows as ascend to Freedom and Landholding. I will take the beast from you, and you will be safe.'

I looked about me. 'But if the danger is so great, why do you wish to take it on yourself?'

'Well, I will have the horse.'

'Then I might as well keep her, if she is worth having, as I have paid for her.'

'No—you do not see. You are a stranger here, and have an air of Innocence about you, and Newness. I can profitably rid myself of the beast without recapture.'

'But I will have neither the horse, nor the profit.'

'What is Liberty worth to you?'

'Come, sir,' I said. 'You will have nothing of me. Not even if you had offered to buy her! I have need of this horse.' And I nudged Tigris to walk on.

Beasley removed his hand from his coat to show me a pistol. 'Oh, just give me the fucking thing,' he said.

My heart jumped into an enormous pounding that made my hands tremble. I had a pistol myself, in fact, but it was unloaded and buried deeply within my saddle-bag. I had, up until this moment, been toying with the idea of declaring myself a Pacifist and doing away with it altogether. Simpleton! 'Take it away, man, take it away,' I said. 'Please, take it away.'

Beasley smiled and settled back into his saddle, bringing the pistol to his waist.

'Point it away!' I cried. 'You will be sorry indeed if you shoot me!' I do not mind reporting that I was fearfully agitated and most dreadfully frightened.

'Certainly,' he said. 'I do not wish to do it. It would be a waste.'

'I mean you will be arrested! There are two Soldiers very nearby—and a Gang entire of the most wretched convicts! They will hear the gunshot and I am sure there will be no escape for you!'

'Oh, there just happen to be Soldiers abroad, just when you need them?' he said. 'That is exceedingly convenient, for your purposes, and not at all for mine.'

'I passed them on my way here. They were digging a ditch, I think.'

'Do I look like a Fool to you?' he asked. The answer was, of course, No, but you do look like a Horse Thief, although I did not say it. 'I did not see a Road Gang, and I was only an hour or two ahead of you on the road. Cheer up,' he went on. 'Some men have got no legs, or have dysentery. And look at you! Two good legs ending in two good boots! And not a hint of dysentery!'

This was madness. Did he want my legs and my boots, too? I slid ungracefully from the saddle and became entangled in the stirrup. As I hopped, Beasley kept the pistol coolly trained on me.

'There,' said I, at last. 'Let me take my things, and I will leave you, and we will part in peace.'

'What is in the saddle-bags?' he asked.

'Nothing of any value,' I said. 'A few poor items of clothing and a water bottle. Mere odds and ends.' It was true; the things of value that I had—my coins, the portrait of Susannah in its golden case, my letter of credit, and the letter I carried for Maryanne Maginn from her elderly Relative, Mrs Prendergast—I carried about my person.

'Where is your money?' asked Beasley.

'I have but little with me.'

'How much?'

'Look here, Beasley—and you see I know your name,' I said. 'Will you leave me with nothing?'

'Show me your things,' he said, and hurried me with his gun. 'I am not unreasonable.'

I was thus obliged to take down my saddle-bags, clumsy with fear, and lay all my possessions upon the road. A pall of sorrow came over me as I beheld this pathetic scene: a pair of trousers; some woollen socks; a shirt; sundry personal items; some tobacco; my water bottle; a deck of playing cards with women in various states of undress and contortion printed upon them, much thumbed, which had been pressed upon me with the harpoons; my pistol, and such. All I called my own in that land, arranged upon the dirt!

As I had prepared to leave England, which I had done at some short notice, I had taken the decision to pack lightly. This was upon the advice of a Reverend who was introduced to me because of his past travels to the Southernmost Colonies. As such, after deep discussion with my father's valet, who was lent to me for the occasion, I took with me one evening suit with tail coat, one morning suit, one afternoon suit, a new gabardine topcoat and my good fur overcoat, which I had had for years but which yet served me well. I brought only one pair of shoes for the evening, and one for the day, and a pair of sturdy walking-boots, one top hat, one broad sun hat, and the usual ties and cravats and personal items, as well as the items for sleeping and the toilette upon which I shall not elaborate. And yet this simple paraphernalia was diminished in one misbegotten night around a card table, after which I limped away with my two harpoons, and only the clothes upon my person and the very poor array described above left to me.

'I will take those socks,' Beasley said, jabbing his weapon at them. 'And the trousers and shirt. And the tobacco. And the pistol. Why did you not have that to hand? You might have shot me, and kept your horse—fool. And the cards. You may keep everything else.'

It felt a disproportionate labour to pack my things once more and sling the bags over my shoulder.

'Pass me that,' he said, indicating the pistol. He took it into his dirty hand and gave it an expert looking-over, his stout fingers amazingly agile on the weapon. 'Have you anything for it?'

'What?' I asked wearily.

'Ammunition? Powder?'

'I have not.'

'What use is it then?'

'At present, it is of no use.'

Beasley lifted his coat and tucked the pistol into his belt. I supposed he would find a use for it. 'Your fur coat is very handsome,' he said. I began to drop it from my shoulders, and he laughed. 'Keep it, you soft ass. You shall be cold indeed to-night. And what are you carrying about your person?'

'A little money,' I said. I did not tell him of the Letters.

'How little?'

I had grown so very tired. I removed my money-pouch and tossed it to him. 'Take it.'

'I had thought to let you keep it also, but very well,' he said. 'Take down these queer-looking irons from the beast's saddle, and you may be on your way.' By this he meant my harpoons.

'You may keep those,' I said. 'I have done with them. I give them up to the Universe.'

'I do not fucking want them, and neither does the Universe,' he said. 'Take them and go.'

I thought I had had hard times in my life before, but that moment was the culmination of all suffering for me: all the broken bones, the cuts, scrapes, scalds and illnesses, the heartache, the loneliness and the fears of my young life had left me standing in the road, rain in my boots, with my saddle-bags and harpoons over my shoulder, watching Beasley ride away, leading Tigris by her reins along the road towards the Chain-Gang and those two Soldiers.

'How do you know the German?' I called.

'I supply him, from time to time,' Beasley shouted back, and saluted me, and was gone.

I released good Tigris in my heart, and consigned Beasley to his fate.

The evening dragged over me. Slow as it was, I was slower still, burdened by bags and harpoons and sadness. What must have been outwardly a journey of some hours stretched into an eternity of torment for me. The sun succumbed to oily clouds, and my heavy step grew heavier and heavier, until at last it stopped, and I turned, and began to plod back the way I had come. I went painfully on, cursing myself with very hard words, until I returned to the place where Beasley had accosted me. I had thought I should have trouble finding it once more, but the handkerchief and undershirt I had abandoned glowed whitely in the darkening shadows. I bent, and took up the encrusted handkerchief, which Mamma had edged and embroidered with my initials in lovely and curling green thread, and turned and plodded once more northwards. I had thought I might wash the handkerchief in the river, but the trees had grown so thick I could scarcely even see it. Instead, I folded the fine white linen as tightly as I might, and buried it deeply in my coat pocket.

The mist coiled and surged around my knees, and the hills shrugged into night, slow waves of darkness blotting out the stars. The rain had softened into a fine mist. Perhaps Mr Green had been incorrect in his forecast of a worsening night.

The stars are friends when one is from the countryside. Or they are reference points, if one is not amiably disposed to the sky. One often has little other diversion in the evenings than to look at them, unless one is excessively fond of parlour games, which I (rightly) am not. And it was the stars on my voyage south that had first truly indicated the strangeness of my journey. Night by night, I had watched my familiar old constellations wheel away and a strange spill flood in their place.

Although I knew it was not there, I looked for the North Star as I walked. Stars are not Indifferent Celestial Bodies, after all, but symbols of all the values and qualities we little persons create for them. I suppose, at that moment, I wished for something constant. Yet all I had were the freezing vaults of the southern sky, silver, green and black, and the moon, a worn coin. Think you the moon is constant? Not at all! The moon is capricious and changeable as—woman! my father would have said, but I do not like him, and am not like him, and so I say: the moon is capricious and changeable as the Economy.

The trees had slowly leant in once more until little of the hills remained. Night's many limbs had unfolded and stretched and filled the spaces between the trees. I could see enough to put one foot in front of the other, but my Cannibal loomed in my mind saying, over and over, You Shall Be Eaten Alive by the Tiger-Wolf, for One. I distracted myself from this terrible fate for a time by furnishing the forest around me with the old familiar trappings from Home. I positioned Mamma's red-and-gold-striped chaise longue by the way up ahead, leaves drifting down onto the silk. As I trudged past it, I said to myself, Well, I could rest myself here, but I have somewhere to be, and so I shall continue on instead. With my mind's eye, I hung the dark portrait of Sir Edwin, my grandfather several times removed, upon a particularly large and gnarled tree, and put the hearth and mantelpiece from the library beneath it. However, this brought suddenly before me a vision of my father, positioned in his great armchair before that very hearth, where he was wont to rest and read and sip brandy in the evenings. The vision of my father gave me such a supercilious look I left off my imaginings at once, with a pang of shame.

I cannot say that the leaves rustled nor that twigs snapped, as one might expect of a wood at night. No, it was silent as any silent thing. In this instance, and as the adage would have it, the grave was the silent thing that happened to come to mind. My hands had inconveniently begun to perspire, despite the cold, and my hold of the harpoons slipped a little. I did not pause to readjust my grip.

It began to seem impossible that there were fellow men of any kind somewhere in this inky wild. Or anywhere in the world! Cold blackness expanded out over the Isle and its rude hearths, across the seas, and subsumed my England and everywhere else, even Spain, until the whole world was night.

When I was a child, I had been afraid of the sound of the beating of my heart in my ears at bedtime, for it had sounded like footsteps in the quiet house, and my young mind had created a frightful man in a black suit who paced in the wall behind my bed. I think he was some deformation of my father. I had not thought of him in some years, but the power of my heartbeat in that quiet night brought him back to me. This did not seem idle fancy, as when I had tried to furnish the forest. He stalked on long legs behind me and tickled the back of my neck. And so there we went, the only two people in the entire world. And one of us was a phantasm. I rather wished to raise trembling fists against the Darkness, but my fists were occupied with the harpoons, and so I began to sing All Jolly Fellows that Follow the Plough instead, which was not quite so powerful as fists. Perhaps there would soon come a path, which might lead me to the station, whatever it might be. I held a flame of hope in my heart that I might come to a cheery sign, lantern-lit, painted with the words WHALING-STATION THIS WAY, ALL WELCOME (KANGAROO STEAMER AVAILABLE), and a great finger pointing towards some warm and friendly place.

It was a silly flame of hope, as so often they are.

Finally, it grew so dark I could not see enough to place my feet surely upon the road. I could do nothing but halt and let the harpoons slip with a clumsy crash. I cast my eyes to Heaven. I had never been quite obsessed with religion, but if I had, I might now have had assistance from above. An Angel might have come, or a scroll with some helpful advice, or a tree might have caught fire, or whatever it is that occurs at such moments.

I felt that the frightful man in the black suit had evaporated, and I looked behind me to assure myself that he was indeed not there. And he was not! A soft glow arose from the trees behind me, and a ball of warm light drifted gently into the sky. Not the Moon! I glanced about to remind myself the cold Moon hung elsewhere above. No, here was a second night-time Body, near and gently flickering—perhaps some extraordinary Southern Star? A sea of leaves rippled golden above me. I cast a perplexed but thankful glance Heavenwards, gathered my harpoons, and made my way for the path, now gently illuminated, which I had passed moments before in the darkness.

My vision of the sphere of light was cut short, for it grew dark once more as I waded into the woods. But I had not gone far when ahead there was the whisper of a calm sea, and a fire with men around: a little spark of home in the land of the strange.

'I had thought you would come to-morrow,' said my Cannibal, looking up from the flames.

I HAVE BECOME QUITE LOST

THE SUN DID NOT RISE, but instead presented as the suffusion of light behind thick cloud, like a flame behind a paper screen. There was a complete lack of shadow and variety. Everything about me glowed with equal import or insignificance, depending upon one's point of view, and whether one was an optimist or not. Ringlets of fog like girls' hair were emerging from the trees and coiling down the bank.

Nobody knows where I am, I thought. Nobody who loves me knows where I am.

Rather freeing, really.

It was cold, and I was alone, except for the tiny figure of a man high on the cliffs at the end of the bay. I stood upon the grassy rise above the sand. I thought of poor Tigris with a pang of affection and wondered where she might be. I liked her better now that we were separated, and I was disposed to think well of her. I had decided perhaps she was a retired carriage horse, her hair rubbed away from long years in the harness. Although she was the wrong colour, her build was akin to my father's Cleveland Bays, which in fact spoke well to her heritage. Dear creature! All she deserved was a gentle Retirement.

My previous night's accommodation had been a very rude place called a 'slab hut' with a fire-pit and a hole for a chimney. Even so, it had been more agreeable than the terrible inn of my first night in the island colony, for at least the hut made no pretensions to anything other than a mean hovel for sleeping in, and did not promise breakfast and then withhold it. My Cannibal had bundled me into this slab hut almost as soon as I had presented myself at the campfire, pausing only long enough to make me quite drunk on rum, which had taken perhaps three cautious sips, and to ask how I had lost Tigris. I believe I delivered a quantity of Lunatic raving about Beasley as my Cannibal deposited me onto the poor cousin of a bed and covered me with a blanket like a shard of ice. It was surrounded by these nice comforts that I had plunged into an embarrassment of sleep. This torpid state had been so profound that after the lapse of hours untold, when it was time for me to awaken, I was in great Confusion, having quite lost my bearings in the stupor of the night. I blinked at the men in postures of repose on the pallets around me and could not at once discern where, or indeed whom, I was.

The hinges had been iced over when I opened the door from within, and I had had to use some force to crack the ice and get out, and thus did I burst forth with a great report and heroic leap onto the empty beach. I hoped I had not awoken the other men. A lone gull hovered above the sand, casting no shadow.

By the hut was another hut, shut up tightly and, by its silence and precarious state of near-collapse, apparently unoccupied. Beside that was a well-made little stone house whose chimney leaked and melted smoke into the white air. Fingers of orange light slid from behind the shutters.

My Cannibal's distinctive head, in shape like a floret of broccoli, presented from behind the slab hut door. The body followed. 'They like to go about their business in there for hours before they emerge,' he said to me, gently closing the door behind him, just as if we were in the middle of a conversation and he were responding to some remark of mine.

'Where?'

'The house. The stone house. Mr Heron's house. He will come and talk to you about buying the station.'

'I do not wish to buy the station, good sir, but only to sell my harpoons,' I said, and became aware as I said it that I did not know the whereabouts of those burdensome items. 'I am pleased to see you,' I added.

'Thank you! Charmed to see you, also.' He said this with a kind of friendly irony about him. 'As to Heron—you will speak to him, nevertheless.'

'I was visited by the strangest vision as I walked in the woods last night, my friend,' I said to him.

'I am fond of hearing of visions.'

'It was terribly dark, and I had dropped my harpoons, and was about to give in to despair, and was even thinking of praying, when a Glorious Little Sun arose above the trees and lit the path for me!'

'Ah,' said my Cannibal, looking disappointed. I gave him the encouragement of an attentive nod, and he went on, 'That was nothing but Mrs Heron's Balloon.'

The fog of the night was now thickening. So much for my floating Platform of a station! Along with the three accommodations I have mentioned, there was a small, windowless building, also tightly closed, back towards the tree line. A little away from the stone house was a construction of some practical use, perhaps a workshop, and a Platform with great cauldrons before.

'What Balloon?' I asked, but my Cannibal was not listening.

The stillness of the place, the cold knifing into my joints, and the weird light, made me think I was rather in a dream. It was the same dream that had descended upon me at the black river. I began to wander hither and yon without real purpose, looking here and there about me. Nothing was of any consequence. I was in my bed in Norfolk, probably, and all my experiences on that Isle were taking place in my sleeping head.

Freedom upon Freedom.

Five large rowing-boats listed together high on the white sweep of sand. Great orange-and-grey rocks nosed and slumbered heavily, piled together like puppies. The waves slinked, gelid and black, a greasy film upon a hollow sea. Hulking great empty spaces lay heavily all up and down the beach, and phantom indentations in the sand warm with the memory of old blood and fat. The cauldrons were gaping seven times larger inside than out, and the boats were curling into themselves for want of use. Spades and knives and harpoons and all the appurtenances of the business were felted with moss. I could feel the ruin of the place seeping into my joints.

And I was come to buy this confluence of empty spaces? It did not seem likely.

I turned to look back at my Cannibal, who surveyed the scene with an air of satisfaction, his hands in his pockets and his head high.

Several coarse-looking men with sacks over their shoulders detached themselves from the tree line and glided, knee-deep in fog, down the bank. Two also carried a huge double saw between them, much like the one with which we would fell trees on the farm. The men did not acknowledge me, even when I stood back to allow them to pass me and go into the workshop. One of their number, an old fellow with an odd way of shrugging his shoulders as he walked, moved from the group and into my Cannibal's arms.

'William,' called another, dropping his sack to place his hands on his hips. 'Your beard astonishes.'

'Aye,' responded my Cannibal through the tears in his eyes, as he gripped the old man with rough and gentle hands.

A grinding filled the air. Someone had begun to sharpen the sawblade.

I moved back towards my Cannibal and the old man. 'What are the cauldrons for?' I asked.

'What?'

'Trypots,' said someone.

'Oh, they are the trypots,' my Cannibal said.

He indicated not with word or gesture but with an air of purpose that we would go together to the little box of a building towards the trees. He put an arm delicately over the old man's awkward shoulders.

'Jack!' he shouted, and there was an answering cry from within. A stinking golden light pooled over the threshold when my Cannibal opened the latch. We pressed ourselves through the stench that made my eyes water and into a simple square room. It was as much a moment of mythic illusion as it had been when I first beheld Tigris in that low alleyway, for there stood a young man pooled in the light of an Argand lamp, posed with a javelin over his shoulder in the manner of a Greek hero. It took no small exertion of my mental faculties to make sense of what I was seeing. The javelin was one of my own American harpoons, and the stinking box was a store-room, lined with shelves and crates and an array of Tools and other Objects.

My Cannibal made a deep inhalation. 'Mark that delightful fume,' he said to me. 'Black oil: our very Raison d'Être.'

He had called the young man Jack. I wondered how this person would disappoint me; Jacks often do not live up to one's expectations. Perhaps that is my own fault, for having expectations of a Jack in the first instance.

Jack jabbed at the air and looked around gravely at me.

'It's no use,' he said. 'It won't fly straight, I am sure.'

He was quite sober-looking, and without the disorder and slovenliness of dress of my Cannibal and the old man, and the other men I had seen outside. His chestnut hair was neatly combed, and his chin shaven, and his dress relatively clean. He was possessed of a calm-looking face, undistinctive, but nicely proportioned, as if an English person had visited a strange country and met a foreigner there who said, 'Sketch me an ordinary young man of your land.'

This ordinary young man stood looking at me with some expectation. I supposed I was now to sell him that which neither of us wanted.

'I have been told they are the latest Technology,' I said. 'From America. I have been told the flue is soft.'

'Yes, I perceive that it is,' he said.

'Well, I am told that is a boon, in harpooning—a soft flue.'

'How could that possibly be so?' he asked. 'Who told you this?'

'The man I got them from,' I said miserably.

'I imagine it bends like a fishhook,' said my Cannibal. 'It would thus contend with the problem of the barb not catching in the whale's flesh, instead slipping out in the course of the chase.'

Jack received this remark with interest, which I was encouraged to observe. Perhaps he had real use for the harpoons. It would be pleasing for them to become useful after having been so agonisingly inconvenient. 'That is true,' he said. 'But does that mean one could not use the harpoon again? Or: if it can be practicably straightened, will the flue not eventually weaken with use?' All three looked at me.

The conversational fog had already descended, as thick and tangible as the fog gathering outside. 'I imagine a smith could easily bend it back,' I said. 'I cannot testify to that, nor to its longevity.'

'You are exceedingly honest,' said Jack.

'Thank you, sir,' I said, with a short bow.

'It was not necessarily meant well,' said my Cannibal.

'It was meant well,' said Jack calmly. He had an air about him of natural command, much like the sailor I had met who looked like Richard III. That person, I recalled, had also been a Jack. Perhaps I was wrong in thinking so little of Jacks; perhaps it was only that my second brother was John, called Jack by many, and often disappointed my young hopes of brotherly treatment.

'We do have a smith. Mochrie would need to see these,' Jack said to my Cannibal and the old man. And, to me: 'How much are you asking for them?'

'How much are you offering?'

'That is no way to do business,' said my Cannibal. 'Father?'

The old man concurred.

'Yes, you must name a price,' said Jack.

There was a brace upon the back wall, stocked with harpoons of a different kind to my own, for these were closer in look to huge iron arrows. I supposed that if my harpoon had a single flue, these must be 'double-flued'. They looked long, long untouched, like ruins in a jungle, sinking into the thick walls of that store-room. 'How much is one of those?' I asked.

'A pair?' said Jack, and he named a price that seemed quite low.

I told him I would sell him a pair of the latest American harpoons for double that sum.

'That is too much.'

'You told me to name a price, and I have done.'

'Well. Indeed. Will you permit me to try them?' asked Jack. 'Mark that I am not agreeing to your price, which I ridicule.' His demeanour remained serious.

'Jack is an harpooner,' said my Cannibal.

'I had discerned that, at least,' I said. 'I will let you try them so long as your man agrees he can restore them to their current state after use. If the flue bends and will not be unbent, they are not of much use to me, and I suggest that, such being the case, you must buy them for the price I have mentioned.'

'In that case, I will buy them for one quarter of the price you have mentioned, for it means they were never much good to begin with.'

I conceded this point, and acquiesced, and Jack absently shook my hand, turning over the harpoon in the light.

'I cannot believe they are for only a single use,' said he.

'No, that would not be reasonable,' said my Cannibal.

'Well, let us have your man look at them, and then we shall see, and you might try them when next you . . .' I trailed off. Go whale-hunting?

A significant glance darted amongst the men.

'Indeed,' said my Cannibal.

'What is the matter?' I asked.

My Cannibal shook his head at Jack, who said, nevertheless: 'It is mid-winter at Montserrat Station, and there has been no whale in nearly a month.'

'I suppose that is not favourable,' I said. Would Jack the harpooner allow me to give him the harpoons? I wished nothing more than to be rid of them.

'Indeed not,' said Jack. 'Once, days were that you could walk from here to Hobart-town on the backs of the whales choking up the sea. Harpooning was like spearing fish in a barrel. Easier! Stabbing fish on your plate with a knife!'

'Yes, and if the fish on your plate were so thickly laid you could not see the crockery,' said my Cannibal.

The old man said some words which I took to mean that Jack and my Cannibal could not remember those days.

Jack flushed quite red. 'I can!' he said. 'I remember them well—although I was a boy—the great seasons when the sea was more whales than water!'

'I allow that I was not here in those days,' said my Cannibal, with his apparently eternal unperturbedness. 'I have heard the stories. From Jack. And Mary. That is all. My friend is a possible buyer, here,' he went on.

I understood myself to be the friend and felt unexpectedly warmed to be named so. I had been lonely, perhaps.

Jack and the old man looked aghast.

'You will buy the station?' Jack asked me.

'No,' I said. 'No.'

'Why have you come all this way? Have you more of these irons to sell—are these a sample?'

'No, I have only the pair.'

'And you have come so far only to sell them?'

'Yes.'

'I am afraid it is not worth such effort,' Jack advised me.

'Well, it is done, now,' I said.

'He had little else to do,' said my Cannibal.

'That is not true,' I said. 'I have a great Purpose here, which I am neglecting, and which every minute I spend thinking about these damned harpoons—please, please forgive my coarseness—is a Betrayal.' My Cannibal had warmed me by calling me Friend, but voicing my Purpose now sent a shard of guilt into my heart. 'If there has been no whale in so long, how will you try the harpoons?' I asked. 'I cannot stay here.'

'It is a question,' said my Cannibal.

'There is no telling how long that may be,' said Jack.

The door swung inwards and a fair-haired young man presented himself, tousle-haired and out-of-breath.

'Seen O'Neill?' he asked.

'No,' said Jack.

'Fucking pot-licker,' he said, and I felt abashed for having begged forgiveness for my far milder uncouth language. 'Only took me awl.' He bowed to my Cannibal and his father, and said, 'Forgive me, O'Riordans. Pot-licker is not a favourable term.'

'It is not,' said my Cannibal. 'O'Neill is in the wood.'

A shout from outside, a man's voice: 'William! Young O'Riordan!'

'That is Mr Heron,' said my Cannibal.

'I am sorry I said pot-licker,' the fair-haired young man said to me.

I had not heard this expression before, and simply nodded in what I hoped was a knowing, and forgiving, way to this young man.

'You are William, then?' I asked my Cannibal.

'William, yes, O'Riordan, is my name. Did I not tell you?'

'You did not.'

'Do I know your name?' he asked me.

'No, you do not.'

'Then it will be awkward introducing you,' he said, and went outside.

'There is an awl here you might use,' said Jack.

'Too big. I need me own awl,' said the young man, and hitched up his shirt to show an expanse of hairy belly, and, below it, the rope holding his trousers up. 'It's better for mending belts.'

Unable to assist in that particular matter, I went outside to meet Mr Heron.

He was a man shaped like a slingshot, his giant bandy legs topped with a little torso. That was all I could see of him until he lumbered much closer. He was red-haired, with beard and whiskers trimmed and tidy. His clothing struck me as rather off for the situation, for he was dressed in a velvet frockcoat, frilled shirt and antique breeches. These items were well-made and well-patched. An outrageous top hat was pressed against his breast. The was something cringing about him, as he reached down to shake my hand, and he fumbled for the words to ask for my name, and then did not ask, for we had not been introduced.

'My name is Fox,' I said.

'I am Heron! Thank you for not minding the niceties,' he said. 'I mean, thank you for telling me your name.' He spoke with the accents of a Northerner; an English Northerner, I should say. There was a trembling about his voice, as though it came from an unsteady place within him.

'We each have a Creature for a name,' I said. 'I wonder if there is something in that.'

'What?' he cried wildly.

'Why, I am Fox, and you are Heron.'

'Oh! Yes,' he said, peering at me like I had said quite the queerest thing he had ever heard.

I looked down to avoid his bright gaze. By my boot, indifferent ants were dismantling a moth. It was likely I was going mad. I had passed one night here and was seeing it by day for the first time, but already I could sense the thick aspic of ennui solidifying the air and suspending the men in a drifting aimlessness. In the time since I had emerged from the slab hut, the beach had been populated, somewhat, by a straggling group of men brought together not by purpose, to my eyes, but impulse. It was clear in their slouching, and their long faces, and their hands like bundles of twigs. There must be some reason we all had gathered there, but I could not get to the heart of it. Oh, whaling, yes, and harpoons, and for me Maryanne Maginn, but these worthy pursuits seemed somehow irrelevant. The men on the beach looked half-transparent beneath their coarse garments, crouching around fire-pits as the sea stretched its fingers along the sand. Some of these men had an English look about them, and some an Irish, and others something else (Spanish, I feared), and one or two others were of the Black Men, yet all were idle alike, and stared alike. I could smell the stench of black oil and sea-rot in the roots of Mr Heron's beard and the stalks of his eyeballs.

Mr Heron was then struck by a wave of social instinct. 'Have you breakfasted, sir? Do you thirst? Are you warm?'

My heart welled with joy at the mention of breakfast, and the words I Am So Very Hungry and Thirsty Mr Heron that I Am Hallucinating Broccoli were rising to my lips, but the wave of social instinct washed away as inevitably as it had arrived.

'Come, come,' he said, and led me by the arm from one sad husk of a place to the next, and never mentioned breakfast again. I was given to understand that now it was Heron who would try to sell me that which neither of us wanted. Ah—the Economy!

The walls crawled with vines, creeping into the brickwork and sending spores into the wood, and coming away dead.

'We occupy three chains of shore and two acres, some quarter—a farthingdeal in the old style, you know—forested with good trees for felling. It is now partly cleared, but I will show you, if you will be so good as to allow me. It is possible to build, although we have five buildings, which is certainly all you will need, unless you have the wish to expand: two slab huts, the stone house, which I can tell you is quite as snug as anybody might wish, the tryworks, which are widely regarded as the best of their kind on the eastern coast. And the whalecraft store, of course, whence you have just lately come. You might even sell the cleared land on to some ticket-of-leave man seeking Freedom from the Panopticon! Now *there* is a profitable notion. You might build a house there, sir, and *then* make the sale. The opportunities are truly endless for the correct kind of gentleman. The enterprising kind, sir, as I can see you are. There is a good freshwater stream. The store is well-stocked with an Infinity of convenient Objects, Tools and Items. And we have five good whaleboats. With a fine shear. See.'

Heron swept his hand in the direction of the boats, the other hand yet pressing his hat to his chest. A yellow-haired man and a native boy-child were sketching shapes upon a hull with their fingers. The child was speckled with green paint and held a paintbrush like a conductor's baton. Tins of paint leant crazily on the sloping sand.

'Is he someone's son?' I asked.

'Well, yes,' said Heron, giving me a searching look, as though inspecting me for physical signs of mental disorder. 'Are not we all?'

'I mean—is he the son of someone here at the station?'

'Oh, indeed. Yes. His father is our smith.'

'I confess I have never met a native.'

'Robert Mochrie is Scottish.'

'That lad is not a Scot!'

'Ah! The lad's mother was native. Robert Mochrie is his father.'

'What are they doing?'

'The American—yon man—has taken up the notion of painting eyes upon the boats. He says it makes for better hunting. Tam is taken with the idea. See there?' And he brought me around to admire the boat they had already painted, with two big black-and-green eyes at the stern. It had an uncanny look to it, like a hollow fish. 'Odd-looking,' he said, in a low tone, while smiling encouragingly at the American and Tam. 'It does not signify,' he continued. 'They can paint eyes and it does not matter. The boats are good boats. The line rides high when it goes. Each one equipped with sweep oar, lances, bails, boat spade, knives, seven or nine rowing oars, two tubs of manila. Not hemp, which becomes limp when wet—useless! All the appurtenances! Irons, of course. That is, harpoons. You will have seen them with Jack in the whalecraft store. Good harpoons. No guns, but you do not want guns, in my opinion. There is a rifle-gun in the house, but I will take that with me. And there are a few pistols for meat. No other guns. And the men are good able men, if you are firm. (Particularly with the Irish. They like to palaver in their own tongue and perhaps make seditious remarks. Popery, of course. Nothing a man can't control.) Good fishing. Sometimes you see an albatross, and that is an auspicious thing.'

I scarcely need remark this persuasive speech was almost entirely Greek to me.

A pale woman in dark dress stood in the open door of the house. 'My wife,' said Heron, and dropped his voice again. 'She is ill. Quite ill, I fear. This life is hard on her. We wish to remove north. Warmer climes. Or Home—but that is colder climes, of course. Odd how it grows warmer the farther north you go, until you go so far you reach the Peak of Heat and it grows cold once more. We have been here some years, now. Some twenty years. She used to live in Hobart-town but grew lonely. And frightened. So she came here. It is bad for her health. She is so delicate. Mr Montserrat founded the station,' he said, changing tack suddenly, turning to gaze into my soul with his blue eyes. 'Mr Montserrat was a true Gentleman—a true one,' he said gravely. 'Very high. Lowered himself to buy the station, but they can be whimsical.' (I took it he meant Gentlefolk.) 'He hired me as Station-Master. And ran into a little difficulty. Personal difficulty. Not to do with the station—we were piling whale upon whale into the trypots. Couldn't move for whale-flesh. Swimming in black oil. Drowning in it. I bought it from him. The station. And now my time here is ended. For the reasons I have told you.'

Mr Heron was growing cadaverous before my very eyes, and his wife was turning invisible.

I looked towards the tree line, where the fog was rising. I seemed to see myself appear, as I had the night before, from amongst the misted trees like an ink stain on paper thickening into clarity.

'What a well-situated aspect,' I told Heron, and he agreed most heartily.

'Indeed, sir, indeed,' said Heron. 'Easterly—best for whales. The head yonder is an excellent natural lookout. There—now, see? Pendle is watching. There is always a man there, watching. Always equipped with the telescope—a sturdy brass Item—which I bought near-new from a Naval Lieutenant of good reputation.' Heron raised a hand to Pendle, who was too far or too occupied scanning the sea to respond.

A few more men had approached, gathered about in some unpolished and silent welcome party. I found I was so disorientated I could not but be honest. 'I have become quite lost,' I told him quietly. 'I ought not have come. I—this place has nothing to do with me. I have gone thoroughly astray.'

'Astray from what?' asked Jack, who I saw had approached, one of my harpoons in each hand.

'From my Purpose,' I said.

'Yes, you mentioned a Purpose. And not the irons.'

'No indeed! I do not care about those. You may keep them. I must return to Hobart-town. I am looking for a Woman.'

'And—the sale of the station—' said Heron.

'Sir—'

I saw the knowledge roll over Heron that I could not buy his station. We cast our eyes together to the clouds and saw the heavy bulk of the absent whales.

'What woman?' asked Jack.

'I beg your pardon?' I asked, but I kept my eyes skywards.

'Who is the woman you seek?'

'Ah—her name is Maryanne Maginn,' I told him. 'She was transported here some thirty years ago, and would now be in her middle forties. Her family wants her.'

'What was her crime?' he asked.

I tore my gaze from the clouds and stared at him. Remarkable question! 'I had not thought to ask,' I said.

'She must have been very young.'

'Indeed. Just a slip of a girl. Perhaps she was innocent of—whatever it was.'

'Or perhaps she was guilty.'

'Only God can say.'

'God, and whatever judge convicted her, and she herself, I suppose.'

'I suppose so.'

There had been a breeze so little I had not noticed it until it died.

If I and everyone I knew were mad, did that not mean all were quite typical Specimens and therefore sane? And it was the right-minded man who was truly the madman, for he was unlike all others?

I once more spied the dim figure of Pendle, watching from the cliff-top.

The fair-haired man without a belt went by. 'O'Neill is exonerated,' he told me. I supposed the men there had need to be fluent in the language of Justice. 'Pendle has me awl.'

'Please forgive Mr Cook,' said Heron. 'He is rough, but he is a good one.'

Jack was intruding upon the painting of eyes at the whale-boats. He vaulted neatly in, my clumsy harpoons delicate in his hands.

'Got a story for me to-day, Jackie?' Tam asked Jack. 'In fact, the fact of it is, I would like a story, if you have one.'

'No stories to-day,' said Jack.

'You can tell me one to-morrow then,' Tam said. 'Well, if you can think of one, which, I hope, that you're able.'

Jack did not respond, but unspooled a length of rope from somewhere within the boat.

'What is Jack doing?' I asked the child, or anyone who would listen.

The old man, my Cannibal William O'Riordan's father, said, 'Putting your harpoons to line.'

I nodded politely, none the wiser, as with all answers I received in that place.

What is the opposite of a vanishing? Mrs Heron un-vanished in the doorway of the stone house, and proceeded down the sand to the tryworks, carrying a lightless sun in her hands. Tam saw her and cried, 'You did not bring the box!'

There was a kind of galvanic quality to the air, signalling that something must occur.

'What is the lady doing?' I asked, but no one was near me. I saw again the little sun that had arisen above the trees to light my way the previous night when it was so dark and I had become so lost.

'It is a Balloon?' I said to myself.

It was quite clear to me what was indeed about to happen—I was not so foolish that I could not read the future in the molecules of the air about me! I thought that I would open my heart to it, when it came.

The watchman Pendle, tiny on the head, was waving his arms. The whistle from afar curled dreamily into my ears. There was a too-far shout. I looked about and back at the head—now empty—and Pendle bloomed into view, bellowing what he would always have bellowed.

'Whale nor-east!'

The men mouthed calls at one another. Heron immediately forgot me and sprinted roaring on his enormous legs with the American for the whalecraft store. The Tam lad sped here and there, all in a dither of excitement. In his haste, he kicked a tin of paint, which knocked over another. A swathe of blue and a swathe of yellow speared down the slipway and slid shivering onto the water. These two colours spread on the pulsing waves and converged, making a ripple of green betwixt them. I saw the image of my miniature of Susannah so vividly in the air before my eyes that I did not need to withdraw it from my breast pocket to confirm the following thoughts: it was not, as I had supposed, that the Artist had not made the painted-Susannah's eyes green because he had no green paint. For her hair was yellow, and her dress blue, and I beheld the phenomenon of the confluence of the two in the paint spilt before me. Artists! They are full of spite. He might have mixed some green paint and depicted her eyes accurately. I made a mental note to pursue a return of the sum I had paid him upon my return Home, or at least to have him paint over the eyes.

The fog closed over. The men had forgotten me, busying themselves, flying into boats. I allowed myself to be carried with the impetus of the place towards a boat myself, the image of Susannah wavering before me. I was glad that I might see a whale, even were it an apparition of our shared consciousness, like an imprecise portrait.

Measureless to Man

THREE BOATS WERE LAUNCHED, FOR it transpired the station no longer employed sufficient whalers to man all five. Ours was last of the three. The freezing waves pushed against my legs and seeped with tortuous slowness through the fabric of my trousers as we waded into the water. I looked up to see the boats that had gone ahead dissolve into the fog. We were left quite alone. I climbed over the side of our whaleboat and seated myself upon a bench. My sensation was, as last night the world had been subsumed by Darkness, now all Creation was being covered by billows of cloud, and our solitary whaleboat was the final outpost of man. It seemed that Pendle had espied the whale just in time, before the great carpet of fog unfurled across the sea.

Heron stood in the stern, his hands tight on a long pole like a gondolier's.

It was so cold I had become numb, which was marvellous. I took my oar and, with the men, began to row into the desolation.

Heron's eyes passed over me, and then passed over me, and then saw me. 'How long have *you* been there?' he asked me.

'Since we departed, of course,' I said, between gasps of exertion, for the water was like toffee, and my arms water.

'Why? Where is Mochrie?'

'I do not know, sir. I simply took an oar.'

Heron gazed above him. His servile aspect was entirely gone, in the boat.

'I do apologise if it is an inconvenience,' I said. 'I had thought you had noticed me from the start. I was beside you when we ran the boat in.'

'No,' he said, and then, 'No sun. It rises over the water, here, and rolls across the sky, and sinks behind the far hills. Not to-day.'

I did not know how to respond to that poetical interlude, and so remained quiet, other than my huffing breaths.

Poor Mr Heron abandoned his impromptu observations about the sun to indicate mournfully how excellently outfitted the whaleboat was, as though he still hoped that I might yet buy the station. There was an excellent lance, and the oars were excellent, the manila he had previously mentioned was also excellent, coiled in an exceedingly well-made barrel, well-fastened now to the American harpoons I had supplied, which were quite the thing, he was sure. And so on. I politely did not listen. He had a compass in his breast pocket, which he had checked once or twice, but now his knuckles were white from clutching the pole.

I was seated starboard with two others. Directly before me was Pendle, who had raised the alarm. I could almost count the lice on his head, pressing themselves close to the coarse black hairs, circling his white bald patch. Before him was Byrne, a young man, not Irish as you might imagine, but brown-skinned, his hair a black mop. Four were larboard: Jack, the old O'Riordan, and two others.

The men rowed as if they were shuffling papers, or dealing cards, or some other effortless occupation.

The four rowers larboard rowed in turn, always with a man resting. Every so often, based on no change of circumstances I could observe other than the passage of time, Heron would make the call, and the rowers larboard would change. We three unlucky starboarders were compelled to row constantly, in order that there were always six men pulling. I had used to row a little upon the lake, at Home, but now, going hard in time with the other men, my body strained and my mind spiralled into the abyss of the impossible reality that I would be rowing Forever in this weird white place.

When I was safely returned Home to England, I decided, I should never go out upon any kind of water again. The passage from Sydney-town to Hobart-town had provided its share of discomforts, particularly on the last stretch, when we sailed directly into a fearsome storm and were churned about our cabins like butter. And yet it was nothing in comparison to the torments of my long voyage from England! I do not know if that ship was a bad one, or if such a voyage was simply always terrible, but I say in full sincerity: may Curses and Calumny rain upon Poseidon! May God dry up all the Seas of the World! For they bring nothing but trouble for any man who ventures out upon them. Mine was a vile journey of several months, of being tossed from floor to wall, and laughed at by sailors, who continually assured me I would grow accustomed to it—in other words, who lied. Inhuman Monsters they were, that they could endure such a life, making such voyages again and again, one after another until they Retired or Died! I had shared a cabin with a Greek called Anastos, or similar. There had been so little space that we were compelled to dress one at a time, with the other lying in his bunk and trying not to get hit in the face by stray socks and braces.

    I had alighted at Sydney-town sick in heart and body. I was to stay with a friend of Mrs Prendergast's, a Mr Halsey. I found that I had to make of myself a nuisance to that man, for no sooner had I presented myself at his establishment than did I fall to the floor and remain quite ill for weeks. And then for weeks more, he made of himself a nuisance to me, by insisting I keep him company, and get my strength back through gambling.

The result of all this was that I had departed England in winter and arrived in Van Diemen's Land in winter, despite the passing of half a year between those two seasons.

Sometimes I feared that all I was really fit for in life was to be wrapped in soft clothing and laid out on a settee. I looked about for someone to whom I might confide this, but I did not see anybody that might do, for none looked as though they had had any acquaintance with soft clothing or settees. Jack was directly to my right hand; he and I of all the men were seated farthest forward. Before him was the jaunty young fellow Cook, who had been searching for his awl, and who then persisted in gazing first at Heron's pocket, wherein the compass lay, and then heavenwards, though there was nothing to see, and back again, as if God might have given him a vision of the needle through the brass case and the leather coat if he longed for it sufficiently. His desire to know where we were was so great it radiated from his very coat, and the bench he sat on, and the back of his head.

'Be easy within yourself, Cook,' said Heron to him. 'We will not become lost.' The words were not intended for me, but I tried to take some measure of comfort from them.

Heron's hands faded in and out of view. They were tight on the pole, his eyes hard on the water.

'What is that pole called?' I asked Jack quietly. 'It is an oar?'

'Sweep oar,' said Cook, with the air of an expert. The whaleboat afforded little conversational privacy.

The old O'Riordan, my Cannibal William's father, sat before Cook. On the forward lean, I saw lumps through the cloth of his back. He was only in shirtsleeves, while the rest of us were in our heavy coats—oilskins for the whalers, and my good fur overcoat for me, which fortunately was spared my ill luck at cards.

Heron called, 'Woolley!' and that man relaxed. Jack, who had been resting, tensed and pulled.

'Never see,' grunted Pendle on the heave, throwing the observation back over his shoulder at me, 'fucking fish in this.'

Jack said, 'We will see it.'

'How large is a whale?' I asked.

'It'll be sixty feet long,' said Jack, and it came to me not in a vision but in a flowering in my gut: a picture of the Leviathan, rolling through the waves.

Pendle laughed. 'You expect a miracle fish.'

'Yes,' said Jack. 'Ninety ton.'

'The largest of its kind.'

'The largest Montserrat Station has seen, at any rate. Mark my words.'

The picture written in my gut started into a tableau: Jack hurling my American harpoons, and the harpoons going wide or short, and the largest whale of its kind known to man and the possible salvation of the station would be lost, and the fault would lie with me.

''Tis the day for the miraculous,' said Heron.

'Why?' someone asked.

'My wife told me.'

'How far shall we row?' I asked, my every word catching in my throat. The other men all seemed quite cool.

'An hour's rowing will take us six miles out,' said Heron.

That was not an answer to my question.

'And, truly, there had been no whale before this for a month?'

'Truly,' said Heron.

'You are a good luck Fox, to have brought us the whale,' said Cook.

'It heard about the fine American irons, and wished to try them,' said Byrne.

This was all terribly droll, I am sure, but in the meanwhile there was perhaps a foot of visibility beyond the hull where I could see a little choppy water, and there was nothing beyond for the eye to rest upon—only thick white fog. Pendle was clear, and murmuring to himself, Byrne indistinct, and silent. Heron had become a ghostly form. None seemed to be afraid.

'Where *is* America, in relation to here?' someone asked, and Jack began some geographical observations in response.

I had seen the Tam lad watching us as we slid the boats onto the water. There was some quality in his face as we went into the blindness that I saw but did not apprehend. 'Oh Jackie,' he had called. 'The fog is not bad. It is part of us because we made it by breathing so much white to-day.'

'Tam is fond of you,' I said to Jack. Although the labour of rowing made speaking difficult, I found I wanted the ordinary comfort of conversation.

'He is fond of everybody, unless he is made to feel differently.'
'He is fond of you,' said Cook. 'He likes your stories.'
Jack shook his head.
'Tell us one,' said Cook.
'No,' said Jack. 'I decline.'
'If you get the whale, tell us a story.'
'Why?'
'It is a bet.'
'Then I ought to tell you the story if I do not get the whale,' said Jack. 'For then I will have lost the bet.'
'Very well,' said Cook. 'And if you get the whale, I will give you a holey dollar.'
'I do not agree to those terms,' said Jack.
'Yes, you do.'
'I shall not need your holey dollar, if we capture the whale. For I shall have my commission.'
'Every man needs a spare holey dollar. Sew it into your shirt, and leave there until you want it.'

Then we were rowing through an icy tunnel of cloud, sharp with the creak and groan and splash of the oars, of Heron's shouts, of hard breathing. Beyond those sounds, I could hear, faintly, some distant roaring or crashing and a rhythmic pulse, and I thought of the Chain-Gang I had seen. I imagined them in a violent coup, pulling out the eyeballs of the soldiers and the man with the whip, the blood freezing in blue jags upon his cheeks.

'Shall we not become lost?' I asked.

'Heron has the compass,' said Jack. 'As he mentioned previously.'

'But the compass will not divulge distance. Who knows how far we shall row?'

'See the light,' said Heron shortly. I did not know he had been listening to our discourse.

'What is the light?'

'Only look.'

I looked directly ahead, astern, past Heron, into the white. Indeed, as I searched with my eyes, I could discern a faint glow through the fog.

'That is where the station is,' he said.

'What is the light?'

'You know what it is,' said Jack, beside me.

'I do not know that I do.'

Four gulls visited our cocoon. They rode the waves, prim with their wings tucked close. An oar dipped too close and they cried, flapped and vanished.

Heron called, 'Cook!' and once again the men larboard changed: Cook, the longest rowing, rested, and the resting Woolley took up his oar.

Pendle resumed his muttering. 'Ninety ton,' he said, whistled, and laughed.

Woolley, who was apparently of a literary disposition, remarked,

'And now there came both mist and snow,
And it grew wondrous cold:

And ice, mast-high, came floating by,
As green as emerald.'

'Wondrous cold it is,' said Pendle.

'But cold and emerald don't rhyme,' said Cook. 'You'd have to say it cald and emerald. Or cold and emerold. It don't work.'

'Take it up with Mr Coleridge,' said Woolley.

"Tis a bold thing for a man who can't say his aitches to speak against the sound of a poem,' said Byrne, for Cook was a Cockney and spoke with a very broad voice.

'HIN Xanadu did Kubla Khan HA stately pleasure-dome decree where HALPH the sacred river ran through caverns measureless to man,' chanted Cook, and was immediately silenced by Byrne, who objected to further poeticism. 'It's a rhyme,' Cook told me quietly. 'And an aitch. Haitch.'

This threat of nostalgia seemed to compel Byrne to propose a new subject for discussion. 'What I wouldn't give for a nice glass of porter,' said he.

'I will join you in that,' said Pendle. 'A pint of porter is your man. A pint of porter and a nice pork chop.'

'And a go on Mary Donnell,' said Byrne.

'Been so long since you seen a woman, you wouldn't know which end was which,' said Woolley.

'Doesn't matter,' said Byrne. 'Topsy-turvy is good enough for this poor soul.'

The men tittered and thence followed a short interval of further hilarity:

'Mary Donnell is an able hand,' said Byrne.

'Aye, she has fair skill at knots.'

'Aye, she can make a surpassing good cunt-splice.'

'And can nimbly use my marlinspike to unknot said splice.'

There the puns failed them, as they had eluded me, although I grasped the general notion.

'And you, Jackie Montserrat?' asked Byrne. 'How will you make use of your commission? Mary Donnell takes all comers.'

'Enough,' said Heron.

'Aye, enough,' said O'Riordan, and remarked something further I did not make out.

'What does he say?' asked Woolley to Byrne.

'I do not know,' said Byrne.

'Is't not your Irish tongue?'

'No, it ain't.'

'Do you consider yourself Irish, Byrne?'

'My father was Irish, and spake Irish,' said Byrne.

'What tongue does your mother speak?'

'She is dead.'

'When alive, what did the dear lady speak?'

'English.'

'Oh aye? What did her mother speak?'

'Fuck off.'

'Aye? Is that the native language hereabouts?'

'Be quiet, now,' said Heron. 'Your sauciness is wearying.'

'She was not from hereabouts,' said Byrne. 'She was from the North.'

'You ought never speak ill of a man's mother,' muttered Cook. 'Especially when she has already gone and Ascended.'

'You should not speak of her at all,' said Byrne.

There was a sudden clatter of resistance against Woolley's oar, and then Pendle's. A second whaleboat spun out of the whiteness and bumped against the hull. Pendle lost his grip; the handle of his oar struck me in the eye. I heard my own voice, shouting, and experienced a moment-long vision of a splintering pane of glass. Yet the pain, after that initial shock, was tolerable, for the cold deadened it. Pendle grunted what may have been either an apology or a gloat.

'Get yourselves together, men!' shouted Heron. 'Mr Fox— apologies. Bear up, now.'

The yellow-haired American was Heron's counterpart in the other boat, standing in the stern with the sweep oar in hands that were blue with paint or cold. He was silently shoving at the water with that instrument, appearing and disappearing in the fog as the boats jostled. The oarsmen likewise came and went. For a moment, I caught the eye of my Cannibal across the water between us. The boats skimmed and dipped and some impression of vaulting skies and seas came upon me and I became dizzyingly aware of the black depths below, and of my fellows and I caught upon a thin film between two abysses. I saw the river-woman of the green eyes serene on her little pony, telling me that the water was deep enough to drown in, and the man with the whip saying drowning was the very nature of water. I came unbalanced where I sat, but hid my swaying by cradling my eye where the oar had got me. The blood was unbearably, unbelievably bright on my fingers.

'Any sign?' called Heron, his voice swimming into my ears.

'No sign,' someone called back, and with a final shove from the American, the boat drifted away and was gone.

It was quieter than before. Through air like syrup I straightened myself and took up my oar once more, but I saw the other men's hands were slack.

'Well, now, we cannot allow those fellows to nab our fish!' Heron exhorted us, his voice ringing into the silence with a vim that was all surface.

'I would allow it, for the prize of not towing it back to shore,' Byrne said quietly.

'Oh come, what spirit is that?' Heron asked.

'The spirit of a weary man, sir.'

'A weary man, Byrne? Or a wicked child? You had best be the former, or I'll put you over my knee and belt you. By God.'

The men sniggered.

'Ready! Heave!' cried Heron, blushing at his own foolishness, over the laughter. I felt such fellowship for him, one Fool to another!

'Come, sir, let us go back,' someone called. 'We will find naught to-day.'

A few men said aye.

'We have our task,' said Jack, and heaved on his oar. The boat pivoted a little.

'Aye, come,' said Heron. 'All hands.'

Silence settled over us once more, until Cook asked, 'Did you ride in, Mr Fox? Didn't see your horse.'

'She was taken from me by a man called Beasley,' I said. 'Do you know him?'

'Why should I know a horse thief?' he asked quickly. 'How long are you here for?'

'I do not know. I suppose I shall return to Hobart-town to-morrow.'

'Afoot?'

'Yes, afoot, unless you have a horse you might give me.'

Cook gave every indication he was searching his mind to think if he had a spare horse tucked away somewhere. 'No, no, I do not,' he said, with what seemed genuine regret. 'I am sorry I cannot oblige.'

'Will you be silent!' said Heron.

There was a bump from below and the boat spun a little again.

'Steady now,' said Heron.

A sleek black back rose and slipped away, and beside me, Jack's oar was shipped and he scrambled forward, and now there were six men rowing, and two standing, one at either end of the craft.

And so the sea yielded the miracle-whale.

'Hard about! Hard about now!' Heron cried in a tight voice.

I was able to crane back and see Jack. He clipped an harpoon—one of mine, indeed!—from its notch and braced his right thigh in a gap evidently made for that very purpose, the manila line hanging from the harpoon over his shoulder. He permitted the boat to support him, with his weight upon his right leg, and his body riding the swell.

The whale drifted. The huge unknowable of the idle movements. Heron shouted for us to heave and we did. I was compelled to turn away from Jack and bend over my oar as the future sprang into two, and then each of those two sprang into two, and on, until what would occur was a great tangled mess of possibility.

'There it is!' I heard Jack shout behind me.

Out of the corner of my eye, I glimpsed the black side sliding beneath the water. It seemed I had seen a flash of eye, but I probably had imagined it. Heaviness settled on me. I had a hand in this, directly, this whale-killing. How could it be right to kill something so enormous and so foreign? Father had championed a practical education for his younger sons, and I had learnt to butcher lambs, sheep, cows, chickens, geese. I had felt that Divinity of Power when a hot and struggling body goes limp in one's hands. And I had hunted for rabbits, and ducks, and grouse, and foxes. I had shot a draught horse with a broken leg, once, with a kind and loving bullet through the skull. But surely if God had seen fit to make a Creature a hundred times my size, and put it in the sea to live, where I could not go without dying, it was not meant for me to hunt it? Had they hunted whales in the Bible? What had become of Jonah's whale? It struck me again that I ought to have made more of an effort at religion, quite in the way I often wish I had paid more attention to arithmetic. Religion might have served me then, in that moment. I did hear another man praying aloud, for God to guide us, or some such.

The numbness had fallen away from me, and my head throbbed. The air had gone from thick to thin, though still white with fog. There was no coastline and no station, out there in the fog, for everything in the world had collapsed. The spectre of Maryanne Maginn fizzed and died like a candle-flame between wet fingertips. I could not see the light over the station.

'She is there,' said Jack.

I could not remember Heron giving any kind of an order, yet we had, as one, ceased in our efforts of rowing, and were occupied in keeping the whaleboat as steady as we could. I was able once more to turn my head and observe Jack, just in the very moment he drew my American harpoon back over his shoulder and hurled it almost straight down, spear-like, with the line diving after. It slipped into the whale like a needle into leather. I saw a tendril of blood that seemed to spiral upwards into the air and hang there, and, with that, the black flesh was gone. Jack took the second harpoon, pointing it uselessly at the empty waves—and tossed it in to sink.

'Why did he do that?' I said, but no one responded. I said, 'He threw the second harpoon away!'

Heron made a dismissive gesture with his hand, then winced apologetically, and made the same gesture once again, but more politely.

Cook whispered to me, 'The two irons are fixed to the same line, Mr Fox,' and I perceived his meaning as the line whispered alive, drawn along by the whale. It whipped, vibrating, back around the loggerhead aft and over the shear, through the chocks and out, humming with friction. The second harpoon would necessarily have been dragged along with this line, and gone over the side in any case, causing us some injury as it clanked by.

Byrne shoved a bailing bucket urgently into my hands. There was smoke rising from the wood where the line thrummed over it, and I leant over the side to scoop seawater and pour it over that point of heat and friction. Steam rose into my face. Delightfully warm.

'Keep it coming!' shouted Heron. 'It will burst into flame if you do not!'

I kept it coming.

'Watch your fingers,' said Cook. 'It'll chop 'em off.' And indeed, the line was singing into the water, quick as a switch.

Heron had abandoned his sweep oar and taken the lance. I was suspended between quiet yearnings that we might catch the whale, and also that we might not.

The miracle-whale sounded. The line made chase.

I resign

I REACHED MY EARS TO the bottom of the sea and heard the great pounding of the whale's heart, and I shot my eyes down, but it was too dark to see. I thought of the great frilled serpent that lived in the black river now so far behind me, and shuddered with dread of the million unseen creatures now swimming and writhing and eating one another below.

In the isolation of the fog, our efforts seemed to me ponderous and strange. I felt as though I had stepped for a moment outside my body, like slipping quietly outside to take the air in the midst of a hot and lively party. I was in this way removed from my own actions, and watched myself leaning over the side to bring water in the bucket, pouring it over the line on the bow and releasing steam, over and over again. From far away, Heron told me to leave off and return to my oar. Slowly, slowly, my body and spirit were drawn together once again. Lurking provocatively at the edge of consciousness was the notion that together we were chasing a fantasy, and our undertaking was that of children at play. We exchanged glances even as we shouted.

Heron lunged forward to Jack's place, and it was like he was wading through melting snow. I had thought his eyes blue, but I did not know they were Electric. Jack drifted aft to the sweep oar. Heron's smart frockcoat caught on the chock, got under the line and was ripped half from his body. He made no sign of having noticed. We heaved on the oars and the whaleboat shot after the line, skimming fast as a dart across the waves. Heron's lance rattled. The prevailing silence was like a force twining amongst us. For the clatter of the lance, and every creak of an oar, and every pant and gasp of a man, the silence parted, briefly, and closed again. Heron's voice was muffled: 'Quickly! Quickly, now, men!'

All at once the tension in the line collapsed, and it slowed and sagged.

'Heave!' cried Heron. Then, as if noticing that each of his vocalisations was sucked back into the quiet as it left his mouth, he ceased to speak for a time.

We worked in interdependent harmony, like fingers upon two hands. I rowed hard, my nerves popping. My shoulders were heavy, even as my skin fair rippled with sensation. We would catch the whale, or not, we would tow it in, or not, and the world would continue, going this way or that, until I died, and then it would go on anyway without me.

Somewhere in Norfolk, a fair-haired girl was forgetting me.

The line moved loosely along the boat.

'We ought to have brought Tam, so that he might learn,' Jack said. 'He is an able little hand, and stays out of one's way. We ought to have brought him for wetting the line.'

'It would be wasted,' murmured Pendle. 'Whaling is a dying trade.'

Just as he spoke, the line slowed again and went slack, swaying with the boat.

'There! There!' shouted Heron. 'Pull!'

He threw his arm back and thrust his lance down into the sea. There was a spurt of blood and he wrested the lance back, screaming laughter, showing his bloodied face. He seemed all eyes then, blue and red. 'Hot blood, lads!' His frockcoat was in tatters. 'Once more!' he cried. 'Once more and she'll be ours!'

The fog was thinning at last and sounds penetrated more sharply. We sped on and, almost all at once, rushed into a cold clear seascape, with waves stretching away, glittering in the sun, towards a crisp horizon. Hair and beards went horizontal.

'Aha!' cried Cook, above the wind. 'Now we'll have her!'

'Is there a calf?' wheezed Pendle. He was red and straining.

'No, no, no calf,' said Heron, who was bouncing from foot to foot, scanning the water covetously, the lance poised over his shoulder. 'Just the lady, just the lady.'

There was a laboured plume, quite close. Heron lunged again. 'Fuck it! Excuse me. Missed her. Pull hard! To starboard, to starboard!'

Again a hearty stab, and again. 'I have it!'

The manila line floated in loops and coils. A brief slick of troubled blood beaded and sank. The miracle-whale sounded once more and the manila was tugged slowly down.

'Steady now,' said Heron.

The water was grey-green and opaque, which was an appropriate representation of the quality of my Understanding in that moment. Due north, the American's whaleboat scurried its oars like a brown beetle. I could not discern faces at that distance; the American's long silhouette was poised at the sweep oar, but the men seated below him could not be distinguished. My Cannibal William O'Riordan was the exception, for his great broccoli of hair was weaving wildly in the wind. There was one other boat about somewhere. Perhaps it was still searching in the fog hanging heavy behind us, south-west, like a curtain over the land. There was a distant shout from the American. With that, the far boat pulled towards us.

'How shrewd is a whale, do you think, O'Riordan?' asked Cook.

'Shrewd enough,' said the old man.

'Shrewd is as shrewd does,' said Pendle. 'It's a buggerin' fish.'

The men directed their remarks with an unnatural attitude, frozen quite still, eyes fixed upon the ocean, glancing nowhere.

'How does it know to come here—just here, of all the seven seas—year in, year out, with its wee ones, if it ain't passing wise?' asked Cook.

'If it was wise, it wouldn't come,' said Byrne.

'If it were wise,' said the old man.

'It is wise,' said Jack. 'For it's not coming in numbers anything near as once it did.'

'This ain't Heron's most beloved subject of talk,' said Byrne.

'Heron cannot even hear us,' said Pendle. 'He's elsewhere in his thoughts.'

We all looked back over our shoulders at Heron in the bow. He was motionless; one leg was propped on the larboard bench nearest him. He gripped the lance in his right hand, speckled with blood, and his left shielded his eyes as he scanned the water.

'Sir,' said Pendle.

Heron did not move.

'I resign,' said Byrne.

'Watch the fucking water, as every other soul in this boat but the two of you is doing,' said Jack. 'I grow weary of your waggery.'

'Oh do you, my lad?' asked Pendle.

Heron stirred at last, though only to tell us to be ready.

'All eyes on the water, men,' Heron said, still distracted. 'We might see her at any moment. She cannot stay below for long, when she is grievous hurt.'

Jack laughed aimlessly to himself.

'Yes, my friend?' asked Byrne. 'Do share the jest. If it ain't too waggish for us.'

But the conversation had exhausted itself. The men fell silent. We gazed out with our wet little eyes, foolishly, as if they were any match at all for the unplumbed vastness around us. The water bounced us like babes on Mother's knee. Gulls cried. The American's whaleboat heaved within easy shouting distance.

'You've pierced the fish?' cried the American.

'Aye, we have her,' responded Heron. 'She's stuck well.'

The American signalled that his men were watching.

Cook seemed to think he saw something, perhaps, and half raised an arm, then dropped it again.

'Is that something?' he asked O'Riordan.

'Aye, perhaps.'

'There—see?'

We were all squinting.

'I see nothing, Cook,' said Byrne.

'There,' Cook insisted, standing, pointing.

'Bloody well sit down, man,' said Heron. 'You're rocking the boat.'

''Tis nothing,' said Woolley.

Cook sat, unsatisfied. After a moment's pause, he said, 'It's her.'

'No, it ain't—'

'Look! Only look! O'Riordan saw it!'

'O'Riordan said perhaps,' said Jack.

We strained, tense.

'There!'

I followed his finger. A blank patch of waves. Then, out of nowhere, apparently: the curving back, hanging suspended and still.

'Larboard! Pull to larboard!' Heron bellowed, but we were already pulling on our oars.

Jack leant on the sweep oar as we heaved and the craft swung and flew. The American pursued. The difficulty had gone out of our endeavour for me; my shoulders no longer throbbed with pain, but instead felt like powerful coils. Jack laughed again, in the icy spray and wind. My thoughts were swept cleanly out of my head. In that wildness, I felt I would be content at that pursuit all day, sighting the whale and flying after it, and me sitting amongst good honest men—or good enough, honest enough—and my troubles smaller because farther away back on that distant shore I could not even see.

The whale seemed a great slug. It was moving, crawling through the water away from us, but continued along the surface. The distance between the whaleboat and the whale shrank fast. Such a spirit of joy I felt that I hoped the creature would dive, and we would be compelled to fly in another direction.

The boat spun too close to the great black back and was bumped hard. Jack and Heron staggered, all laughed.

'She's got spirit in her yet!' shouted Byrne.

Heron lanced the waves wildly. The creature had gone.

The American's boat pulled close.

'She cannot truly sound, not hurt as she is,' Heron assured us or himself. 'She is about.'

In his own whaleboat, we heard the American shout for William O'Riordan to ship his oar and take his place forward with the harpoons. 'If we see her, we shall pierce her,' he called to Heron.

'Aye, good,' called Heron. 'Put some distance between us, man. Let us cover a greater area. Pull north.'

The boat receded.

'We shall have her before them,' murmured Heron. 'She's close, she's hurt, and she's ours.'

Indeed, the whale rolled her side above the water not even half a cable-length away south-west, which was aft, back where the air was thicker and where somewhere in the fog there was land and the station. I perceived that no other man than I had yet seen her. I remained silent and watched her labour a time and sink.

The great tail came up and then the others saw her, first Woolley, then all. She could not stay down, it seemed; her sleek head bobbed up and the plume sputtered.

'Hard about, Jackie!' shouted Heron. 'What are you standing there for? Hard!'

Jack gave a silent and mighty pull on the sweep oar and we rowed, swinging the boat hard to larboard and shooting off anew.

The whale writhed, sank and rose. At Heron's command, we heaved and held on the oars. The boat sidled up to the whale and bumped her, and she bumped us. The American's boat appeared once more, and we heard his growing cries.

'There ain't a call for another iron,' said Byrne. 'Stockworth ought to come forward with the lance.' I gathered Stockworth was the American's name. 'Mr Heron!' called Byrne. 'The lines will grow tangled if we introduce another harpoon!'

Heron did not hear, or else chose to ignore him. 'Death throes!' he cried. 'This is it, men. Here it is.'

Cook excitedly uttered some nonsense about calling for the priest.

'Silence now,' said Heron, steadying the lance.

The whale presented her harpooned flesh; the instrument was indeed hooked well, and the line looped and trailed about her in the troubled waves. Even then, at the moment of crisis, Jack and I exchanged a quick glance, to indicate the sentiment, Well, fancy that. It is a good harpoon, after all. I observed its handle jutting out, swinging first above and then below the water, and felt the phantom shape of it in my palm. My fingers clenched on the oar.

The American with his whaleboat was close, then, and I imagined I could hear the hard breathing of William O'Riordan, who took aim, tense and certain.

'William O'Riordan is a very able harpooner,' said Jack. 'Abler, perhaps, than I myself.' A sudden and visible jolt of competition gripped Jack. 'Mr Heron!' he called. 'You must prevent O'Riordan from harpooning the fish!'

'Aye,' said Pendle. 'It will become a fine mess. Bring Stockworth forward with the lance.'

I did not care about a fine mess. I willed the whale to sink once more into invisibility.

In the far boat, William O'Riordan flung the harpoon sharp and sure towards the whale's side, but the whale indeed vanished below, and the harpoon sliced into empty water. 'Ha!' cried Jack. Hand over hand, O'Riordan pulled the harpoon back. He shook salt water from the cold iron.

There was a mighty shock to the whaleboat and Jack's knees failed. He buckled and was flung from his feet. My own oar was wrenched from my fingers by the same great force, and I found myself cradling the prostrate Jack. Someone's fingers were pulling at my shirt. I looked about wildly.

'Where is she?' shouted the American from afar. 'Hold steady, we'll find her!'

Woolley and Heron were rolling about in the bilge, somehow. An enormous spout showered us and there was a second great crash. Jack's hands scrabbled uselessly to gain a hold. He gripped my flesh for a moment—soft muscle—a wet shoulder. I caught a glimpse of the elder O'Riordan's bare feet, of Pendle's head. Wood splintered, and next I was in a tangle of flesh and cloth in the ice-cold sea.

It had never been a dream at all.

No one will give me a straight answer in this place

WE HAVE QUANTIFIED TIME BY dividing it up into the convenience of hours and minutes and seconds, but we do not know—or at least we do not generally know—perhaps Mr Newton knew—anything at all about its innate qualities. How is it that a moment is finished almost as soon as it begins when spent in the company of a loved one, but the same span stretches and drags when we are in pain or peril? This is a phenomenon so woven into the fabric of our days that I had never before thought to question it, although when I form it into words, it does seem something the Scientists must have pondered.

There was a man clutching and scrabbling at me, pulling me down, and a great pressure was building inside my chest. I saw a flash of the man's face distorted in animal frenzy, and it seemed a dreadful oil painting I could examine at my leisure. It was the amiable Cook. His eyes were bulging and red, and his mouth, so close to me, an enormous cavern jutting with sharp white rocks. His hair speared from his head this way and that. I was thrashing my legs in the wildest of gavottes, preoccupied with a dread of the whale rising beneath me and swallowing me, and the need to rise myself, and the desperate need to breathe. Yet Cook wished to wrestle with me! His ghastly face was suspended before me, growing huger and huger until I could see my own scream reflected in his pupils. Outwardly, it must have been seconds, but inwardly, this moment extended into infinity.

My fur overcoat was a further hindrance, and I slipped my arms from its capacious sleeves. Cook had it in great fistfuls, which caused a strange scene indeed: when I let it go, he took it, and it was very much like he was my servant, helping me from it, and would swim away and hang it somewhere discreet. He wrestled with it a moment, and then seemed to become aware I was not in it, and let it go.

Our heads burst above the surface. I attempted to shout at him to be still and calm, but I could only gasp in a ragged breath as he clasped me urgently once more. We plunged under once again, and as Cook was dragging me down, I was dragging him up—he had me by the hair, and I had him by the rope he wore as a belt—and therefore we moved neither up nor down, which is in accordance with some Physical Law or other. I thought, very clearly, that if I lived, I should buy a book of the works of Mr Newton and understand them once and for all. I would scour his Indices for mention of words like Suspension, and Time, and perhaps Prisms, and master the physical world in which I was then struggling to live.

In that state of Scientific suspension, Cook had become some beast frantically casting about in an alien medium for something, some gift of purchase, some intuition of direction. Now it seemed to me that he was spinning and spinning in place, but still somehow holding me with an unshakeable firmness. My breath, which I had been holding once again, jumped like a living thing from my lips, and a great stream of silver bubbles spiralled before my eyes. They seemed faceted like jewels, and I saw long-familiar faces in each of a million surfaces.

I do not reveal this lightly, and I do not present any ameliorating details, but I tried to give it up, to save myself and cast Cook away. Although we both wished to live, we had become at odds, and were causing one another to die. But Cook latched on to me, climbing me, twisting around, as though he might stand upon me and get his head above the water in that way. I was thrust deeper. I felt like I was full of my mother's embroidery needles, which were coming out through my skin, and they were pulling a bright rainbow of silk threads from me, but every time I tried to snatch a breath of air, the needles were sucked inwards and burrowed into my lungs, and the silk became a great tangle. Perhaps I deserved it. My father had always said that we all get what we deserve, in the end. Somewhere there were unintelligible voices crying, high and shrill, like the screeching of imps, and a terrible booming, all exceedingly muffled. I felt hot, although somewhere in my rational mind I knew I was in fact cold, and with that thought I became cold indeed. Out of my chest came a wordless exclamation against death.

Then, all at once, Cook became tender and soft, and drifted gently to the surface once more, pulling me with him. I could not compel my body to swim upwards; all I could do was cling to Cook and rise into a great black shadow. We bumped against a wooden structure that went on for many miles in all directions. Cook's face brushed my own, his eyes and mouth now loose and amused, and his fair hair shifting. He was very white in the dark below the whaleboat. My heartbeat throbbed me into a realm of a clear blue medium, where I saw refracting light making a cathedral inside my eyes, and my mother's silk threads untangling and weaving themselves into a mathematical design, and I heard a high and humming song.

In Xanadu

The hull dragged against me and I was pulled sharply sideways and upwards, where the air whipped at my face—sweet air, most likely, presumably fresh and wholesome, and yet my lungs simply would not breathe, no matter how I willed them. My arms tightened convulsively until I was strangling Cook, but Cook's face remained calm and happy. Extraordinary, really, to have one's head above the water, and one's body below. My ears were as closed as my lungs. There was a cacophony of sound occurring somewhere quite distant and separated from me by many layers of some thick matter resembling blancmange. I distinguished the characterful voice of my Cannibal, not by any particular words he was saying, but by the deep and resonant sound of it, coming from his chest and passing into my own body by means of Vibration.

Boom boom boom!—was my Cannibal's voice in my bones.

I thought I should prefer to live in the world, for it is a known quantity, and there is no guarantee of Paradise. I had certainly not attended Church as faithfully as I ought— although Hell held little terror for me, after the torment of the voyage from England, and the dreadful inn in which I had stayed my first night in Van Diemen's Land.

I breathed, and my lungs convulsed, and I coughed and could not breathe again but spewed water in nightmarish quantity. There was coarse stuff rubbing against the side of my face. It was my Cannibal's hair. His arms were wrapped about me, and we were afloat, and I was holding Cook's neck, and Cook was bobbing dead with us.

The air ripped at my throat as I breathed and breathed again, and found that I might continue breathing, and that I most likely was not Dead.

'There now, Fox,' said my Cannibal William O'Riordan, 'I have you.'

I thought, with pleased surprise: He has learnt my name.

*

As I was hauled into the American's whaleboat, the gunwale pressed into my gut and I spewed again, but not in so great a quantity, and it was not seawater but a sour white mucous. (That is perhaps unnecessary detail.) The American and another person had me under my arms, and they pulled me in, where I lay back across the benches, retching and wheezing. Both O'Riordans were there, sitting up, soaking wet, looking grave but calm. Pendle, too, with his head in his hands and another man's coat over his shoulders. I closed my eyes and tried to still my body, but I could not—my teeth chattered, my hands shook and I breathed in great gasps like the tearing of Heron's frockcoat. Water slopped beneath me. Men above me were saying things, as men do, and the boat tilted. More slime sputtered out of my lips. A great wet something was laid next to me. I opened my eyes to look at the sky, and then rolled my head to the side to meet the eyes of the corpse.

'Mr Fox,' said Pendle, 'what is that in your hand?'

I found I could not speak for the chattering of my teeth.

Pendle prised my fist open. I do not know why he was so curious, but I could not have told him, even if I had been able to speak, for I had been completely unaware until that moment that I was holding anything at all. In my hand, like a little drop of sunshine, was Susannah's portrait in its golden case. Pendle wordlessly closed my hand back around this item. 'We're movin', Mr Fox,' said he. 'Come centre with me. They must row.'

I do not know how, but I found myself sitting looking about me and more hands took me and helped me slide into the middle of the seats, where the elder O'Riordan and Pendle were, dripping and blue, and where Cook lay, arranged with a bench running beneath his head, and his back, and his buttocks, and his knees, and his feet, that he might not sag into the empty spaces and down into the bilge where water shifted and pooled. It was jolly fortunate Cook was proportioned precisely as he was, and fit along the benches so well, and I tried to say this, but my teeth simply would not cease their chattering.

Someone settled a heavy coat around my shoulders. It went some way to the beginnings of comfort, but what I really wanted was a pair of warm arms encircling me. There was a quiet shuffling and organising of men. I came to see that Jack was seated near me, wet and grey with cold, and quaffing from the rum keg. He clamped the back of my head and pressed the keg to my lips. The rum began a slow fire in my belly, which I quietly vomited down my chest. Jack assisted me to take some more. How we destroy ourselves!

Behold the wreckage of our expedition, and the pointlessness of it.

'Not pointless,' said Jack, and I supposed I must have uttered that last thought aloud.

As one, the men began to heave home.

I began to think with some compunction of my mother, and worry that she was not comfortable in the attic of our house, although we had furnished it quite commodiously, and had all agreed that, had she been in her right mind, she would certainly have wished to withdraw thus from Society, and not let her distracted state be generally known. At least, Father had told us that we all agreed on the matter.

I thought of Aunt Jane, my mother's sister, a woman who had always had the expression upon her face of someone who has just remembered some important thing she has neglected to do. Jane had visited every week—no small feat, as she dwelt most of the year in London—and asked to be allowed to see Mamma. I wondered if she yet persisted, and if Father had yet permitted this, or if he was still of the opinion that Jane would only create in Mamma an agitation, and do her ill. I saw Mamma, in that moment, quite vividly, as I had left her to come away to the colonies. She was a sober woman in a plain grey dress, her dark hair under her cap, sitting by the dormer window with her hands folded in her lap, and her eyes looking at something I could not myself see, until they shifted to meet my own. Her apron was creased, which Father had taken as a clear sign of Madness—as she had always been an exceedingly orderly person—but was, I admitted to myself there in the boat, merely a sign of being denied servants beyond the Giantess Betty Sikes, or a flat iron.

She was much changed. Only such a very short time before she had been put away had she been lively, and full of intelligent talk, and ornamented, and coiffed, and dressed in the proper array of costumes for the proper times of the day.

'Goodbye, Mamma,' I had said.

'Goodbye, Gabriel,' she had said, and looked away again.

There in the rescue-boat, Jack said, 'They must be drowned.'

'No,' said Pendle. 'Only Cook.'

'No,' said Jack. 'Heron and Byrne. And Woolley. Where are they?'

I found it difficult—impossible—to think of three more deaths. The cracking of the hull of our whaleboat was still tormenting my ears. Starboard I could see it, half-sunken, one painted eye sticking up on a jagged piece of wood. It was like—well, I do not know what it was like, for it was entirely outside my experience, and I could not liken it to anything. Unless a cracked walnut, perhaps.

A water cask bobbed upon the waves.

'What does it signify now Heron is dead?' asked Jack. 'Does Mrs Heron own the lease to the station?' Jack lowered his voice and addressed me directly. 'It would not be preposterous if Heron had willed it for sentiment's sake to me, you know, for the sake of my father, who founded it and sold the buildings and the lease to Heron before his death.'

Whose death—Heron's or Jack's father's—I did not know.

'I heard a man call you Montserrat,' I said, the rum at last stilling the chattering of my teeth enough to speak coherently.

'Yes, indeed. I am John Montserrat, son of George Montserrat, of Montserrat Station. But I do hope Heron is not dead,' he added, and it was simple in its sincerity.

In that moment, we both became cognisant of the third whaleboat, only some short distance to larboard, but back and away where we had to turn to see it. The helmsman of that boat was a Scot whose name I did not know. He was not Mochrie, Tam's father, who was some other person. This man stood very straight at the sweep oar, presiding over the men with a solemnity suitable to the occasion. And there they were: Heron, Byrne and Woolley, ranked down the middle of the benches between the rowers, other men's coats on their backs. All three were certainly yet living, although sitting with their faces like the lurid masks of actors depicting unhappy Ghouls. Heron's gaze was fixed upon some unseen object in the water, and I further contorted my body and the scales fell from my eyes to see the whale floating huge and dead. The harpoon in its side was still and steady, and the line trailed from it and dipped neatly below the surface of the sea. Beside the harpoon someone had pinned the whale with a red flag on a wooden spike, and the Creature drifted in pillows of fog like a black lump of an island claimed for the Nation of Red.

'What is that flag?' I asked.

'The waif,' said Jack.

'No one will give me a straight answer in this place,' I said. 'No one will say, That Thing has This Name, and it has a particular use, and I shall briefly describe that use to you, and I hope that will fully answer your question.'

There was a pause, and then Jack said, 'That thing is called the Waif, and its purpose is to mark the Carcase, so we might find it again later.'

'Thank you,' I said. 'And what are trypots?'

'They are like to cauldrons, and their use is for rendering the whale oil.'

'Thank you. And—what is the matter with Mrs Heron and Balloons?'

'She makes little Hot-Air Balloons out of paper, and sends them up,' said Jack. 'Tam likes to assist her. She teaches him.'

'Thank you.'

Despite the numbness of my skin, I could still feel the phantom shapes of Cook's hands clutching at me.

'Forgive my abruptness just now,' I said. 'I think I am rather upset.'

'There is nothing to forgive,' said Jack. 'I am rather upset, too.'

The light, like the beacon that had guided me in the night, was hanging yet over the station. Below it, the station itself was a little painting in black and white, touched with yellow, as we heaved into view of it. The fog was entirely gone on shore, and on the water it had loosened its great mass, persisting only in plump little billows, here and there. Ahead I could see the white sweep of sand and the waves worrying at the grey rocks. Mrs Heron was standing with young Tam, watching us come in. She held a string attached to her little sun, which was indeed a miniature Hot-Air Balloon. Central to the tableau was the stone house curling smoke from its chimney, windows alight, curtains drawn, with the other buildings dotted about it. The wall of trees lurked behind it all, and the cliff meditated, just as much as any living thing might meditate. I did not know if I had killed Cook, nor how I would be judged.

Ashore, Mrs Heron stooped slowly and gave the string to Tam. The lad stood, gazing above him at the glowing Balloon which, I suppose, served as a kind of North Star, for it did not waver.

I am not claiming we are Princes

WE HAD DRAWN ASHORE AT the station, which must have been as we left it, in substance—and yet it had changed. I cannot define the nature of the change, but it was to do with the mood of the place, or its spirit. No longer was the station a decayed hulk with my person at its centre and a gaggle of hopeless waifs radiating raggedly out like the spokes of a rusted wheel. Probably that had been some breed of Narcissism, or vain hope, thinking myself the centre of things. Now, after I had been humbled by the sea, I saw more truly. Now the men went with purpose, performing various necessities with a grave brevity, while I was catapulted out into some obscure sphere of uselessness. I moved to stand by some men who were preparing a great fire upon the beach, but I got in their way, and so I withdrew to look out at the sea. Susannah had been wearing dark watered silk the last time I had seen her, and I saw that dress now in the waves. Time grew sluggish, once more.

Jack had given me some clothes. He was a shorter man than I, and my ankles were cold, although the rest of me had warmed sufficiently.

A slender young man I had not seen before came from the slab hut to stand beside me and join me in my idleness. This person was of tidy appearance, grey-eyed and clean-shaven and with neatly cropped auburn hair. He had his hands in his pockets, and we tarried like two visitors to an Exhibition to look together out at the great black body drifting amongst the rumpled silk of the waves.

When I was a child, I was known as the Careless One amongst my family, for once in 1827 I had forgotten to close a gate behind me. In consequence, a bull escaped and was shot by a neighbour for his Menacing Ways, which embroiled my family in a feud with the neighbour's family. Thereafter, I was not trusted to perform the simplest of tasks alone, and was given cheap dishes from which to eat, lest I somehow sweep them clumsily from the table in the ordinary course of dining. In fact, I was not at all Careless. I was a lad of ten years, and had not shut the gate because I had been stung by a bee upon my eyelid, and could scarcely see, and was rushing inside to show my mother, or anyone who might care.

I felt almost entirely convinced I had made a good effort to save Cook's life, and had not abandoned him to his death, nor caused it through Carelessness. I made this remark to the young man beside me.

He did not respond, and in that moment a great clatter arose from the whalecraft store. I had no occupation to busy my hands, and no useful destination where I might go. We went together to the whalecraft store, which seemed to grow smaller the closer we drew, as the forest rose up around it.

In the store was a great chest of tools with a scratched brass plate marked MONTSERRAT affixed to its lid. Jack was scrabbling within.

'Do they belong to you?' I asked Jack.

'The tools? No—Heron's.'

'Did he purchase them from your father? It is only that I see the box is marked with your name.'

Jack did not respond. He was sorting through the tools, and, reaching the bottom of the box, sorted through them once more.

'What are you looking for?' I asked.

'The broadaxe.'

There was a thud against the door. 'Open, Jack,' someone said. 'We are bringing him in.'

I obliged by opening the door.

Woolley and Byrne were bent under a great wet cocoon.

'The women have stitched him in,' said Byrne.

'Why is he still wet?' I asked.

'He ain't,' said Byrne.

I gazed at the flowering patches of damp scalloping the shroud. 'Why are you bringing him in here?' I asked, just to see what contrariness I might receive in response.

'Animals can't get him in here,' said Byrne.

'The tiger-wolf?'

'Yes, as an example. What are you looking for, Jackie? We want to put him on the chest if you will close it.'

'The broadaxe,' said Jack.

'Why do you need it?'

'Why do you think?'

'He doesn't need a coffin,' said the clean-shaven young man beside me, and I realised that it was my Cannibal.

'I did not recognise you—William,' I told him. I did not wonder at his transformation, for I saw how he had frowned, and squared his shoulders, and reached to doff a hat he did not wear when the men had brought Cook in his shroud. It was Respect.

'I know.'

'Did you save me from drowning?' I asked him.

'I did,' he said. 'But I could not save Cook.'

'Neither could I,' I said. Never had a more useless exchange been made. There Cook was, dead and sewn into his shroud, and my Cannibal and I hardly needed to tell one another that we had failed to save him. And yet somehow it seemed it had needed to be said.

*

Clouds bellied the roof of the stone house. The Herons stood leaning upon one another, Mr Heron about three times his lady wife's size, but each looking as ill as the other. An old woman lurked behind them in the doorway, a long white rope of hair over her shoulder. She was clothed in black, but wore an unexpectedly gay shawl crossed over her breast, in white and red. I saw—real as you like—the words KANGAROO STEAMER picked out in chimney-smoke above her head. I thought I could just about remember a day when I was not hungry.

Mrs Heron clasped a grey shawl over her hair and around her shoulders, and, all in all, with her little shoulders and her sorrowful face, presented an appropriately tragic figure for the men gathered before them. Well, I was also a tragic figure, with my black eye, and my empty stomach, and my fear that I had perhaps strangled Cook to death in the waves.

Mrs Heron looked at Jack, and then beyond him, and pointed. Heron's top hat lay discarded in the sand. Jack had unhappiness rolling off him and pooling about his feet, but he took the hat, and brushed the sand from the silk, and tried to give it to Mrs Heron. She would not take it and instead indicated her husband, but Heron did not notice Jack at all, and so he was left holding it, and his unhappiness meanwhile rolled and rolled on. 'I need the broadaxe,' he said.

Pendle gave a start.

'What? Come, man!' Heron said. 'Come.'

'I never give back him his awl,' said Pendle.

'What?' Heron demanded.

'Cook's awl,' said Pendle. 'I borrowed it and never give it back. He told me he wanted to mend his belt, and I put him off, for I had not finished with it.'

'Well, there is nothing to be done for that now.'

Jack came to stand with my Cannibal and me. 'I wish to build a coffin,' he whispered.

'I know; be quiet, now,' said William O'Riordan.

Jack still had Heron's hat; he turned it over in his hands. Tam was roaming the edges of the group, mouth fixed in a silent grimace of pain. I supposed one of the men gathered must be Mochrie, the boy's father, but it was Jack who extended a hand to him. Tam came to be comforted.

Farther along the sand, the fire had come to life. Sparks spun into the lowering sky.

'Stockworth, take who you will,' said Heron. 'That is, do not take any who went into the sea; who you will besides. The whale is not lost,' he added as an aside to me, of all people—and I remembered he had wished me to buy his station. Did he still hold out that hope? 'We have marked it.'

'With the Waif?'

'With the Waif, Mr Fox, yes.'

'Finnegan, leading oarsman,' said Stockworth. 'Evans, O'Neill, Costello, Landry, Featherstonehaugh, Gilbert.'

'What are they doing?' I asked William quietly.

'Going to bring the whale in.'

'Retrieve both irons,' said Heron. 'They are the property of Mr Fox.'

William whispered something in a wet rush in my ear. I did not follow his meaning at all, but pretended that I had.

Heron made a sidling movement and seemed to prevent himself from saying something. Then, with a glance at Mrs Heron, he said it regardless, but with such painful awkwardness nobody could quite look him in the eye: 'Well, I will say that Mr O'Riordan the younger demonstrated proper courage in leaping into the waves to come to the aid of those wrecked.'

There was a moment of sombre nodding at my Cannibal William, who said, 'Thank you for saying it, Mr Heron, but I must remark—it was only natural I should have left the boat as I did and go to the aid of my father, who cannot swim, but also, I must say that Mr Fox here made a truly valiant attempt to assist Cook to stay afloat. Instead of seeking immediate safety after the wreck, he placed himself in yet greater personal peril in order to preserve Cook's life. Indeed, it was witnessing this struggle that caused me to leave my boat a second time, after my father was secure, in order to go to their aid. And I wish to observe most emphatically that it is through no fault or negligence upon Mr Fox's part that Cook is dead, for he did all a man might be expected to do.'

The ignoble wrestling-match below the water flashed before me, and I felt Cook's fingernails in my skin.

'Well, I acknowledge you, Mr Fox. And I thank you. This Accident is most unusual, and we generally keep very well here. Montserrat Station has never before seen a man die. Except for—well, a man who deserved death, long ago. Mary, will you feed the men early to-day?' Heron said, directing this last question at the old woman in the doorway. 'We will have much labour on the morrow. Do not become too drunk,' he added to the group at large.

'Sir?' said Woolley. 'What about Cook?'

'I have not yet decided,' said Heron. 'We have never lost a man before to-day,' he said to me, apparently unaware he was repeating himself. 'As I have previously indicated, Montserrat Station has always been exceedingly Safe, as well as Profitable. My thinking now is that we bury him here—'

'But we have no priest, nor graveyard.'

'We might send to the village . . . someone of us might go to-morrow. They have a priest to say the proper words.'

'Cook was a Catholic,' said William. 'There is no Catholic priest there. We should have to send someone farther afield.'

I was quite consumed and felt I had speak. 'Why did you say that, man?' I whispered to William.

'What?'

'That remark of yours, about how I tried to assist Cook. There is nothing to what I did. He was beside me in the water.'

'They ought to know you tried,' he said. 'They are all of a kind, and you and I are of another kind—Jack Montserrat perhaps with us—and they do not quite trust us to be amongst them.'

'What kind are we?'

'Why, gentlemen.'

I looked at him in great astonishment, and yet there was some truth in what he said—with his hair trimmed and beard shaven, and his modulated voice—Irish in the way of Mrs Prendergast, cultivated with that same Refinement and Learning—he could, perhaps, be a gentleman—except that he was a whaler in the far end of the Empire!

'I am not claiming we are Princes, but, never minding our present circumstances, we do both come from better things than this, I think,' he said.

This seemed a reasonable remark. I supposed that, even as he was presently a whaler, I was an Harpoon Salesman, and if he were good enough to not deem this ungentlemanly, then I should not mind the whaling.

'That old man—is he your father?' I asked. 'Forgive me, but . . .' I could not think how to phrase my question without offending my Cannibal William forever, but the moment was gone. The old man was a rough sort, and the lumps I had seen through the back of his shirt spoke to a brutality of floggings.

'Cook was a God-fearing man,' Pendle was saying.

'And there's Mrs Cook and the wee Cooks,' said Woolley. 'How should you have them told? Shall they be so far from his grave?'

'This man had a family of his own?' I asked.

'Aye, sir, three children,' Heron said.

'Where are they?'

'In the town, sir, with their dam.'

'That is, the village?'

'No, that is Hobart-town.'

'Well, they will certainly wish to inter their father's body in the proper manner.'

'There is no ship due until the end of the season, Mr Fox,' said Heron. 'We had a ship once, you know, the *Tristessa*. A splendid craft. She operates out of Hobart-town harbour, now, and might be bought back, by the enterprising gent. And to take a corpse by horseback—what, we should have to lash him like game over the horse's rump.'

'And we do not have any horses,' said my Cannibal.

'Yes, that is a more pertinent point,' said Heron.

'We ought to row him south to Hobart-town,' said my Cannibal. 'That, to me, is undeniably the most practicable—and correct—solution.'

'I do not know that I can spare the men,' said Heron. 'The whale will be brought in this evening. It is not that—it is not that I do not wish to do well by Cook . . .' he said, and let his words fail there. For, of course, it did rather seem that he wished to do better by the whale than by Cook.

'How many men would such an undertaking require?' I asked. 'Really, Mr Heron—and I do hope you will forgive me—I beg you to understand that I am driven to appeal to you thus only by the strength of my natural and sympathetic emotions, and speak therefore plainly and humbly as one man to another, and trust that my entreaty will be accepted in this same simple spirit—I urge you to do things in the proper way, sir, despite the inconvenience it will evidently cause you.'

'One man could do it,' said William. 'I will do it.'

'I certainly cannot spare you for as long as it would take you to go alone,' said Mr Heron. 'Why, that would be a fortnight or more! And you only just returned from your visit to the Police Magistrate in Hobart-town.'

'Six men could make it quicker,' said Pendle.

'Yes, Pendle is correct,' said William. 'Six men could do it in three days. One day for rowing, one day for rowing back, and perhaps one day there, to see Mrs Cook and to deliver the body where she directs us.'

'There is naught we might do on the matter to-night,' said Mr Heron. 'Mr Fox, I take what you have said in the same spirit you gave it, and, further, I thank you for it. Mr Stockworth, go for the whale now. Before it grows dark.'

'We will take a lamp,' said Stockworth, the American, looking at the sky. I thought of bearded and haloed Mr Green back in the Royal Hotel, looking to the sky for guidance.

'It is fortunate the fog has cleared,' said my Cannibal, as the group dispersed.

'Yes,' said Jack. 'I can see the beast from here.'

Heron made as if to depart, but his wife stayed him, and murmured something into his ear.

'Mrs Heron,' said the man. 'Allow me to present Mr— Gabriel?—Fox, of . . .'

'Norfolk, madam,' I said, and made a humble bow.

'Do come inside for a drop of whisky, Mr Fox,' said Mrs Heron, speaking to me across a distance of a hundred thousand miles, and at that same distance I followed them into the stone house.

'We do not stand on ceremony here,' said the lady, as Mary met us at the door and showed us directly into a kitchen-cum-dining-cum-drawing-room.

Three glasses and a decanter upon a small table sparkled in the firelight, set out at the ready for us, a great greasy fingerprint besmearing the rim of each glass. I supposed this hospitable setting was in anticipation of my presence. There were two chairs, but Mary obliged us by bringing a wooden stool from the hearth, and Mr Heron further obliged by insisting his wife and I be seated while he perched.

'Jack Montserrat made this stool,' he said, as if to explain his wobbling.

The room was simple but not Spartan, with some small concessions to comfort. Chief amongst these was a large painting hung upon the far wall, the work of an Enthusiastic Artist who had perhaps once seen a horse in a dream. The walls were whitewashed, and the hearth scrubbed, and the fire banked. My hosts nicely made me welcome, with much gracious gesturing, and Mary poured us some whisky, and then took down a fourth glass and poured some for herself, and withdrew to drag a wooden box from an obscure corner and into the warmth of the hearth. She sat upon this box and swilled her whisky. Though she was an old woman indeed, parchment-skinned and claw-handed, her eyes had the brightness and sharpness of youth, and she moved with fluid ease.

'Fancy a bite o' mutton?' she asked me, with an air more conversational than deferential.

'Thank you, but if it is not your usual dining hour, I shall not impose.'

'You must be truly famished, Mr Fox,' said Mrs Heron. 'We shall all take a bite of mutton, thank you, Mary.'

God Bless Mrs Heron! Mary arose from her seat and set about bringing down an outrageous quantity of Items.

Mrs Heron was a woman perhaps in her middle forties, and thus about the age Maryanne Maginn would be, if I were to find her living. Her hair was neatly put away under her cap, and her golden-brown eyes seemed to take up half her face. To my homesick self it seemed those eyes cast a soft light over her features, making gentle shadows in the creases and folds in the skin of her face and at her throat. I missed my mother. Mrs Heron did seem ill; she was thin and drawn, her hands like trembling Autumn leaves. Not leaves: the skeletons of leaves, after the fabric of the plant has decayed, and nothing remains but a tracery of veins, fine and frail. I learnt long ago from my father that it is unmanly to express sentimental feeling, and so I did not, but all I could see was my mother alone in the world.

'I am afraid you are hurt, Mr Fox,' said Mrs Heron, gesturing to my face with her unsteady hand.

I thanked her and told her it was not bad.

'It must have been a distressing thing,' she said. 'Dear Mr Cook was a good, simple, salt-of-the-Earth Christian soul. You did very well to try and help him.'

I responded that I had done little enough.

There were some more such niceties, which I am afraid I did not pay terribly much attention to; I had already partaken of a great quantity of rum, in the whaleboat and ashore, and now the powerful twin forces of whisky and nostalgia were having a deleterious effect upon my ability to discourse. I had made careful study of *Dainty Conversation for the Drawing-Room: a Guide for Young Ladies and Gentlemen* when my mother had given it to me, but there was no passage within dealing with how one would approach my particular situation, drunk and post-catastrophe, conversationally speaking.

The Herons were Northerners. Mr Heron told me he was from York, and Mrs Heron named a village I did not know as her native place. They had first been introduced at a public meeting for the New Christian Society of Earthly Fellowship. The lady had an air of social smoothness about her, and I could picture her in some comfortable salon, engaging in polite discourse. Her father had been a vicar, she said. She and Mr Heron had come to the colonies as missionaries, where, due to one or two misfortunes, they had rapidly exhausted their funds. He had got into whaling as a temporary reprieve from impecuniousness, which had become a permanent reprieve, and thus, twenty years on, she found herself in a place very unlike Home. The long and the short of it all was that she was desperately ill and unhappy, and was leaving Mr Heron, and would return to England. I did not know at all what to do with this information, but the Herons were quite calm.

'That is another reason why my husband must decide to do the correct thing and send six men to take Mr Cook to Hobarttown,' she said. 'That I might go with them.'

'You need not go so soon,' said Mr Heron.

'What would be the good of delay?' she said. 'We have spoken of this already, Edgar. We have agreed.'

'Think of Tam, if you will not think of me,' he said, with an earnest passion. 'Will you leave him, the motherless one, with no comfort? No maternal bosom for his head?'

'I am not his mother,' said Mrs Heron stiffly. 'Do not say such things to me. You cannot know how I shall miss him.'

'You need send only five of your own men, if I join the party,' I said, encroaching upon this delicate matter like a man stamping about in a forest made of eggshells. I regretted already that I had spoken. 'I have perceived you are anxious not to lose so many hands,' I continued. 'And you have seen I am able enough to row.'

Mr Heron looked deeply sad. 'Thank you,' he said. 'That is helpful.'

'Mr Heron will follow me, as soon as he has sold the station,' said Mrs Heron.

'Have you many prospective buyers?' I asked them.

'You were the first,' Mr Heron said.

'I was not a prospective buyer.'

'Still,' he said. 'You were the first one.'

It was at this moment that there was a tap at the door.

Mary reared her head up and around from the pot she was tending over the fire. 'No, missus,' she said. 'You have not even had your mutton.'

Indeed! Mutton was the chief concern. Mary was a woman who could see into my heart.

'Let him in, Mary,' said the lady.

With a wordless shrug that communicated very precisely, On your head be it, missus, Mary opened the door to admit Tam, the native child.

'There is no need for this, Leah,' said Mr Heron. 'The boy should be outside.'

'There is every need,' said Mrs Heron, rising, and so we all rose.

Tam sidled up to the hearth, where he delicately began to draw the wooden box from where Mary had put it.

'Won't you accompany us, Mr Fox?' Mrs Heron asked me. 'We are going to launch our Balloon once more, for the aid of the men going to fetch the whale.'

'One can launch too many Balloons,' said Mr Heron.

'I do not know what you are trying to say,' said the lady. 'I do not know if you are speaking literally, or if you are insinuating something Other, something Greater, but I am not terribly interested at this moment in metaphors and abstractions. Mr Fox. Tam. Let us go.'

Our last Balloon sadly caught fire and then sank

A TINY WHALEBOAT SCURRIED ACROSS the water to the whale. It crested a wave, and seemed to grow hazy, and double. Were there two boats? And two whales? No. I was drunk. I mustered my powers to focus upon the task of seeing straight.

The red flag they had pinned upon the beast flickered brightly against the exhausted day.

'It will soon be dark,' said Mrs Heron.

Some distance from us, men sat around the fire upon the sand and passed bottles amongst themselves. Someone's solemn voice reached us, singing a song about a woman with diamond eyes.

'We send a Balloon up every night,' Tam told me. 'Or day. Nearly every night or day. To-day it is twice.'

'What a charming practice,' I said, with the precision of the careful inebriate.

'I suppose it is,' said Mrs Heron. 'It has become our Habit. It is an effective beacon if the men are at sea, but of course, they so rarely are.'

Tam hushed her fiercely, and she gave him a smile.

'It does not matter if we are frank about the state of things,' said the lady. 'Mr Fox is not a buyer. Anyway,' she added distractedly, 'you ought always to be honest.'

'Oh yes,' Tam said, and settled the wooden box upon the sand to draw out a quantity of folded paper—letters, it seemed.

'And you sent it up to-day, when we went to sea,' I said.

'Yes,' said the lady.

'Indeed, I believe you sent it up somewhat before we went to sea.'

'Perhaps—I cannot quite recall the precise order of happenings. But I sent it up so that you—you all—might see it. We make do, here,' she went on, showing me the folded letters from the box. 'Once I had silk! That was long ago. We use paper now. Our last Balloon sadly caught fire and then sank. Tam and I have constructed this one out of some letters I have received over the years.'

Tam eased the folded paper open into a china-fine sphere heavy with handwriting. The ink was black, green, brown, and some parts of it were cross-written. Long joins disturbed these letters; I could see that the papers had been cut into Elliptical pieces and pasted together to make the globe. The work was so surely and tightly done that there were no holes in it at all, save for a round opening at the base of the Object.

'That is how my sister writes, when she has much to say,' said Mrs Heron, indicating the cross-writing. 'She is very frugal. I suppose we are frugal, also—aren't we, Tam? We make use of the materials we have to hand, thus.'

I was still rather caught on the idea of a humble missionary having silk. Hardly frugal!

'My husband bought it for me,' she said, when I made some enquiry. 'When I first expressed the need to make a Balloon.'

The *need* for a Balloon!

'I have seen a Balloon,' I said. 'Before now, I have seen one. In London, launched from Hampstead Heath.'

'That is interesting,' said Mrs Heron, and delicately withdrew her attention from the conversation.

'Was it greater than ours?' asked Tam.

'Yes! It was so large a man and a woman were lifted up by it.'

Tam looked brightly at me, and then up at the sky. 'I wish to launch a Mouse, but Mrs Heron says it is not good to do.'

'It would be bad luck for the Mouse,' I said. 'He should not be able to steer. Do you know where Hampstead Heath is?'

'London,' said Tam.

'Very good.'

He looked at me as if I were a fool. 'You *said* it. Moments ago.'

Well—true. Why was I persisting in my attempt to talk to a child? Evidently, I was not doing it well. 'Should you like to visit London one day?' I asked him.

'No!' he said, and turned his eyes to the Balloon.

To my dear one, I read upon the sphere, and *the elm is in blossom*, and *I pray nightly*, and *her son is making some reckless choices, and she needs comforting*, and *I cannot abide by cambric for that particular purpose, whatever you say*, and *how I miss you*, and other ordinary intimacies. My mother had written me such things, when I was in London and she at home. This before she was shut away.

The true value of a social letter had never really struck me until that moment, as I gazed upon the Balloon writ all over with words that, between them, amounted to: I remember you, and I wish you to remember me, and here are some of my thoughts and daily happenings, that you might hear and see me, and have me closer to you. And I desire the same from you.

Please respond at yr. earliest convenience.

'Where is your mother?' I asked the child.

'Where is your mother,' he said. It was not clear if he was quoting me in disbelief at my further stupidity, or asking me, or something else, but he did not pause to explain. 'We write twelve names here, every Balloon,' he continued, indicating the inner surface of the sphere through its low opening. Here and there, I could see words written in red ink in the empty spaces. My vision blurred and flowered again at the eddying currents of script.

'For the twelve Apostles,' I said.

'No,' said the lady.

I looked about me for William, for I was struck anew with the sensation I had latterly felt that he might assist me through every strange encounter that I did not quite understand. I could not see him, although I gazed at the faces of the men singing and drinking around the fire. And yet, no matter that the conversation was half unintelligible, I possessed in me the peculiar need for the comfort of talk, and thus went on.

'Did Mr Newton write of Balloons?' I asked the Ballooning duo in general.

'Sir,' said Tam.

'Yes. Well done,' said Mrs Heron.

'I beg your pardon?' I asked.

'Sir Isaac Newton,' said Mrs Heron. 'Not mister, as you have said. And in answer to your question: I believe Sir Isaac Newton lived somewhat before the Balloon, and therefore no, he did not.'

'Ah—thank you.' I lapsed into silence once more as I racked my brains to recall whether I had referred to the great Scientist as Mr Newton to anybody in speech, and therefore embarrassed myself. I could not call to mind an instance of this, but still I felt uneasy.

'What is to-day?' I asked.

'Indeed,' murmured Mrs Heron. She and Tam had drawn some other Items from the box and were working quietly together to fasten the paper sphere to a tin lamp of some rustic design, with a long white string coiled below. There was a simple harmony, and a quiet companionship, about their work.

'Forgive me—no. What is the date?'

'Oh, I see. It is the thirteenth day of July, I believe.'

'It is a Wednesday,' said Tam.

'Wednesday's child is full of woe,' said Mrs Heron. She said it without thinking, as some say 'God bless you!' at a sneeze, lest the sneezer die of plague.

'I was not born on a Wednesday, so that is not me,' Tam told me. 'On what day were you born?'

'I do not know,' I said.

'I do not know either,' said the boy. 'Only that it was not Wednesday.'

'It was a fine day, whichever it was,' said Mrs Heron, and she and Tam exchanged a fleeting smile. Her attention to him was simple and motherly, and their manner together more natural than mine had ever been with my own mother.

Mamma had gone into the attic the previous December, on Boxing Day. She had been there now for six-and-a-half months.

The sea before us rustled like writing-paper.

Once Mamma had removed her bonnet on a social call where it was not appropriate, and had subsequently stayed quite some time longer than was polite. The lady Mamma had been visiting on that unhappy occasion had complained to her husband, who had gone so far as to report it to Father at the Club on a London visit. Instead of dismissing it as the trifle it no doubt truly was, Father brought it home with him, and we were compelled to address it *en famille*. That had been an embarrassing discussion for all but Father, I think, who delivered a Lecture for Mamma's edification, leaning back contemplatively in his chair.

I do not know if that had been the beginning of Mamma's doom. The seasons rolled on, each one sparser than the last. Perhaps it is more likely that it was simply one thread in a tapestry which, when all such threads were skilfully stitched together, made a picture of the attic door. Mamma and I had never discussed it, but once, privately, she had given me a certain look, and I had pressed her hand in a certain way, and thus we communicated our mutual understanding—I think that is what occurred. It must have been lonely, that slow death she suffered of discreet exclusion from all the kinds of things that happened: the salons and balls, parties, soirées, Informal Gatherings of Friends, dinners, luncheons, picnics, Charitable Visits to the Poor and, in short, all the diversions that add texture to a gentlewoman's days. Lonely too must have been the understanding at home that it was her own failing that caused it. And had I ever indicated with the merest positioning of my own body that I participated in this careful and courteous expulsion from Society?

I hoped I had not.

It was rather hypocritical of Father, I thought, to bear so heavily on the conventions of Society, and hold Mamma to such account. He himself preferred to remain mostly retired, excepting the Club, and any engagements he could not get out of. Well—despite the antiquity of our family and our house, Father was, after all, merely a Baronet. This might impress the villagers, but could hardly impress anybody who was anybody. Perhaps, then, rather than be Unimpressive, Father stayed away. A startling idea! That instead of holding himself separate because he felt superior to the foolish mores and inhabitants of our social circle, he would hold himself separate because he felt inferior!

I had thought it best not to dwell on such things. For how can such a quiet and subtle Mechanism as Society be approached? What can one do?

'Silence descends,' murmured Mrs Heron. Indeed, all conversation had stopped, and even the men at the fire along the beach had fallen quiet.

'I was thinking of my father and mother,' I said.

'What of them?'

'I do not know—it is difficult to say.'

I felt my own failing, and perhaps weakness, more keenly than I ever had before. Now so far removed from that Society, it actually puzzled me that I could have been so weak, and for what reward?

'It is incredible to me—extraordinary that we—People—occupy so narrow a plane!' said Mrs Heron. 'We go along the ground, and skim across the water, when all above is the vast chamber of the Sky—and all below the vast chamber of the Sea! Oh, do not mention miners to me,' she added, as an aside to Tam. 'They do not go so very deep. Have you the match?'

A look of raw longing flashed across Tam's face. He produced a palmful of matches from his pocket and sifted through them to select one which to me looked identical to the others, but which had evidently distinguished itself somehow to the child. He struck it against the lamp and touched it to the wick. We all shifted our feet a little as the Balloon glowed, the words writ here and there all across it now transcendent. The Balloon trembled and departed Mrs Heron's hands, and she let the white string run through her fingers. A still and silent picture of the line hot from the whaleboat and slicing into the waves passed before me. I watched the Balloon rise and rise, until it could rise no more, for Mrs Heron had closed her hand. The little craft hovered benignly above, drifting like a boat in the current, anchored to the lady. We looked up at it together.

'I have caught a little Mouse, for the day when Mrs Heron says yes, we may launch it,' Tam told me softly, as we gazed above. 'He is called Tam. That is what people call him. But his name is Thomas Mochrie.'

'Is that your name?'

'Yes.'

'And how should you like to fly?'

'Fearful!'

'You are fearful?'

'Flying is fearful! I should be very happy.'

The men on the water had conquered the Island of the Nation of Red, for they had taken down the flag, and had harnessed the whale, and were dragging it back ashore. They moved so slowly they seemed not to move at all, except that if I looked away and then back again, they were nearer. I looked then back towards the house, whence Mr Heron had emerged on his preposterous legs to watch the whale brought in. In the moment I saw him, however, he was looking not at the whale, but at the Balloon. His face was peaceful with wonder.

'Like a Chinese lantern,' said I.

'What's a Chinese lantern?' asked Tam.

'Why, it is something like your Balloon. From China.' I hoped he would not ask me more, for I had never seen a Chinese lantern, only read of one. He looked a little like he might enquire further, but Mrs Heron spoke instead.

'Will you certainly join the party to Hobart-town to-morrow?' she asked. 'It was kind of you to offer, and, of course, it will be the most convenient mode of delivering you back to civilisation, such as it is. And you spoke so well in favour of taking Cook home to his family.'

'Yes, I will, if Mr Heron so decides,' I said.

'He will so decide.'

Tam had grown quite still, and he now looked from the Balloon to Mrs Heron. 'So, you are really going away?' he asked her. She put a soft hand on his shoulder, and seemed about to say something, but did not.

I looked from the Balloon to the lady and child together and then out to sea. The whale startled me with its closeness; Mr Heron and some others had come to wade out and help draw her in. Night had fallen, and the fire leapt high, and the men bore lamps, and the Balloon circled above us all. Limp and dreadful was the whale amongst all the glimmering.

We had been at table, in the wreathed and garlanded Hall, and we had vanquished already many rich courses, and had shored up against Linzer torte and plum pudding with custard. Through the windows it seemed evening had fallen already, as it so often does on Wintry afternoons. It had not snowed that year, not yet. The snow would come soon enough, bringing with it the end of birdsong, and the sacred hush of the white drifts.

Our crystal shone in the gentle candlelight. The glossy holly leaves wound about the candle-sticks seemed more orange than green. Sir Ranulph and Lady Oxford were each serenely holding forth, he on the topic of the Christmas Sermon we had latterly endured, and she on some matter relating to the South of France. Father sat, speaking but little, nodding sombrely and surveying us all with a proprietorial air. Sir Ranulph was at Father's right; Lady Oxford to his left. Other such minorly distinguished persons glinted and chattered about them. Mamma was arranged at the foot of the table, looking pleased and quite merry, conversing animatedly with Mrs Pilkington. Susannah Prendergast, at my side, was gowned in the colour of ivory. I could hardly see where the silk ended and the skin began. At Church she had worn a nicely festive hat, modest enough for the occasion, but with a gay Tartan ribbon. Now there was a heartbreaking little comb enamelled with a woodland scene in her hair.

This easy and familiar tableau represented not a small success on the part of my family. Mamma had been out of favour for some years, and for us to have gathered an even somewhat well-connected party of personages on Christmas Day really did augur well for Mamma's social recovery. When extending her invitations, she had represented it as an intimate gathering of our nearest Friends and Relations, thrown together in the merry spirit of the season. As such, our manner was peaceably gay. In reality, the occasion was an iron-clad military campaign, and we were advancing as one upon the well-defended Fortress that was Society.

I had put it to Susannah that it would be well received if she would sing later, and she was telling me she sang only Indifferently—which I felt sure must be modesty, not truth— and she advised that I ought to ask Mrs Pilkington. *That* lady sang like a Nightingale, and would certainly be kind enough to oblige us, perhaps accompanied by Miss Georgiana on the pianoforte, she said.

The general conversation reached a natural lull, and into this Lady Oxford said, 'Apphia, my dear, what is this curious Pastry before us? It is so charmingly done.'

Mamma gave an engaging little description of Linzer torte, and how that Viennese delicacy came to be upon our table every Christmas-time by way of Mamma's maternal line, who were Viennese themselves. This last remark was made very humbly, for it was well known that the Viennese line to which Mamma referred was grand indeed, comprising many lofty Personages. Her description was necessarily directed at all seated, for in order to answer Lady Oxford's question, Mamma was compelled to address her across the several places between them.

Father cut her off after perhaps a minute's speech, by saying, 'Dear Apphia, it is not Viennese at all. Anybody can tell it is named after the town of Linz, in the north.' With that, he began to tell Lady Oxford of something entirely unrelated to Linzer torte or Vienna.

Susannah's guardian, the Ancient and Terrifying Mrs Prendergast, radiated ominous feeling from opposite us. Into the shocked quiet, I rather desperately made the suggestion that, if Susannah were too shy to sing alone, she might try a duet with Mrs Pilkington, adding that we had received some new and quite charming airs from London only perhaps a fortnight before, including a duet or two, that she might look at. Or she might try a duet with me; no matter how she felt her voice might be lacking, she should be glad of my accompaniment, for I was so terrible that she would be Angelic by comparison.

Susannah seemed reluctant to resume our talk, for she still looked somewhat appalled at Father's dismissive words to Mamma, but she correctly, I suppose, put those feelings aside and said, 'I am not shy—do you not know me at all? I am merely sensible, and sensitive of my particular talents, or lack thereof, in this case, and really had better not sing.

Why do not we not play a round of cards instead? Mr Fox and Miss Georgiana will no doubt join us, if we ask.'

It was at this juncture of our conversation that we both at once became aware that the general susurration of conversation had fallen away. Instead of this chatter, we came to hear my mother's voice, though not loud, as she listed my father's many failings, and her feelings on the matter. Into the now ringing silence, Mamma had quite calmly said down the table to my father that he was an ungenerous man, and that he was unkind, vain and boring, and she was sick to death of him, and that Linzer torte may be from Linz originally, but was well loved in Vienna too, and many other things.

My father lowered his fork back onto his plate and left it there. I felt cold shivers of dread come upon me so forcefully that my own fork clattered from my hand.

Mamma rose to her feet, her green-and-white silk rustling like a bird's wings. She looked young in that moment, as if I had been granted a glimpse of her before she had married my father. Her dark hair was usually quite grey at the temples, but the candlelight shone in such a way that it became golden-red. Her eyes gleamed. There was a great and clumsy bumping of chairs as the gentlemen rose with her—I too; not Father—only for her to tell the party at large: 'I find this life quite unbearable, thank you.'

Susannah had looked and looked at my mother, little pink spots in her cheeks, where most others looked down, or discreetly out the windows, or at the ceiling, or anywhere but Mamma. I willed Susannah to look at me, but it was very likely she had forgotten my presence altogether. Freddie, standing with the other gentlemen, seemed frightened.

Mamma did not weep later, nor beg forgiveness, which is what really sealed her fate.

'It is what she would have wished for,' my middle brother John told me, after Father had shut the attic door, as though she had already died.

'And what of your return to England?' asked Mrs Heron. 'Will you also be sailing soon?' And so we stood, amiable and polite, conversing Englishly on the shore of the edge of the Known World, at a station afire with hope and grief and queer private Symbols dancing about in people's heads.

'I should dearly love to go Home, but I cannot,' I said. 'I have a task here I must complete.'

'Not to sell your harpoons, as I have been told?'

'Indeed no, madam. I am in the colony on behalf of a lady who has sent me to find somebody who was brought here thirty years ago.'

'Brought here?'

'As a convict. But her Relative is very respectable.'

Mrs Heron received this information with a thoughtful silence, but when she next spoke, it was of another matter. She did strike me as an intuitive woman, and perhaps somehow she had discerned the connexion, for she said: 'I heard you were clasping the image of a young lady when you were pulled from the sea. May I see it? And know who she is?'

I had Susannah's miniature in my pocket, for I had resolved never to be parted from it, and I gladly brought it out to show her. It had not suffered at all for its immersion; in fact, it seemed a little brighter than before. Mrs Heron passed the string of the Balloon to Tam, just as I had seen her do some hours previously, when I was brought back to shore in the whaleboat. She took the portrait in both her hands, letting it nestle in her palms like a precious thing indeed.

'She is a very pretty girl,' said Mrs Heron.

Tam asked to be shown the image, and, upon looking, concurred that she was indeed pretty.

'Her name is Susannah Prendergast,' I said, 'and she is the girl I shall marry.'

'Is it a good likeness?'

'The likeness is fairly good, although the Artist made her eyes grey, when they are in fact green—I had thought at first that perhaps he did not have any green paint, but as you can see, her hair is yellow, and her dress is blue, and it would be a poor Artist indeed who did not know one might combine those two colours in order to make green.'

'It is perhaps more likely you have misremembered the colour of your young lady's eyes,' said Mrs Heron. 'You would not be the first young man to do so.'

I was appalled at this suggestion. Yet, as I gazed upon the little painting of Susannah in the fey and flickering light, and then remembered the girl herself, I had to admit that—yes, perhaps her eyes were truly grey.

'And she is waiting for you to complete your task?'

Now I found I stared at Mrs Heron, for she asked me something that I had never actually put into words. 'I hope so,' I said at last, after an uncomfortably long moment. 'After she refused my suit, her great-grandmother, Mrs Prendergast—who is her guardian—summoned me and charged me with my mission, which is as I have told you, to seek this person—whose name is Maryanne Maginn—and bring her Home.'

'Ah! You say Susannah did not agree to marry you.'

True! Yet I believed that it was my own poor timing that had caused her to decline my advance. The awkward aftermath of my mother's withdrawal from the table, and the delicate concession that the party was concluded untimely early, and the stolen moment behind the curtain—I had acted wrongly. 'She did indeed not agree, but only because I had timed my proposal very poorly.'

'And Susannah will agree to marry you, if you are successful?'

'That is my most earnest hope.'

'So the last word you had on the matter from the young lady was to refuse you?'

'Yes—'

'Forgive my wife,' said Mr Heron, sweeping towards us like a man half sea, half flesh. 'She has been long without anything new to read.'

'Do not dismiss me so,' said the lady. 'It is a serious matter—the matter of marriage—and I do not think Mr Fox begrudges a kind and maternal word from an older person than he. Young men, in general, do not know the gravity of wedlock—of what they ask. You are asking the young lady to surrender her dignity to you,' she said to me, 'and her security, and to commit her body to pain and peril, and if she has told you that she will not, I do not know that it is quite correct of you to try to convince her she is wrong. You will forgive, I pray, such frank words, for they are kindly meant.'

I thought of Susannah as she had been that Christmas Day, soft in look but firm in tone. And I remembered her pale gown, and skin, and shuddered to think it striped in blood, and that rosebud mouth agape, and the eyes—green, or grey, I did not know—wide. Why should I think of blood! What images Mrs Heron conjured!

'I have borne and lost twelve children, Mr Fox. So you see I do speak with some authority upon the matter of a wife's suffering.'

I looked at her and thought: My father would lock you in the attic for that.

A profoundly intimate question sprang to my lips, for it was a matter I had pondered in the past, when my friend Georges Aubert's two sisters both died in the same accident and—I blame my inebriation—I asked it. 'How does grief function, Mrs Heron, in the heart, I mean, when one grieves more than a single loss? Does one feel each loss as keenly—are two deaths twice as painful as one—or does one have a Limit, beyond which one cannot grieve anew?'

Mr Heron grew a little more cadaverous, and Mrs Heron a little more translucent. 'For me, it was grief multiplied by twelve,' she said.

'Grief upon grief,' said Mr Heron.

I had the sudden and quite desperate need to withdraw, and go and be alone somewhere, and get yet drunker, and perhaps, finally, eat. I stepped away too hastily, and made my apologies, and forgot to thank the Herons for the whisky, or to delicately enquire if the invitation had been purely social, or if there was some further matter they wished to discuss with me—in short, I fled.

'I look forward to seeing you with us in the boat to-morrow,' said Mrs Heron, a dozen times bereaved, to my receding back.

I had looked at the Balloon too long, for twin beacons were burnt into my eyes, and drifted ahead of me as I went.

It was never thus

I WAS IN THE LIBRARY in conference with Dr Hughes, my brothers and Father when came the summons from Mrs Prendergast.

Dr Hughes was a squat man of similar dimensions all the way around, his height and width being about equal. All the hair had been frightened from his head and into his ears, which rendered him half deaf, for which reason he abused an ear trumpet.

Father stood warming his backside before the hearth. He was a remarkably grey man, and had been so all my life—and earlier, as I judged it from portraiture—neither growing older nor changing in temperament in any way. Some men grow fat, and some become wasted, and some more conservative, and some more liberal with age—not so my father. I believe he was born Finished. He swept with evident ease and comfort through life, allowing all its vicissitudes to bounce from him along the way. He had a profusion of thick grey hair very neatly combed and oiled with Macassar, and a similar thickness sprouting from above his large eyes. He had a vertical line for a nose, and a horizontal line for a mouth, and a high forehead, and everything, every aspect of this man's face and person, was the same grey as his hair. That evening, before the library hearth, his hands were clasped behind him to lift his tails, that the heat might more directly access his seat. Although he was addressing us, he was directing his gaze out of the window to the clouds pregnant with the snow that had not yet fallen. Everything about him—the easy attitude, the mild arrangement of his features and the loosened tie—spoke to a distinct air of contentment.

It was Boxing Day.

'Given that we are all in perfect agreement on the appropriateness of this measure, for Lady Fox's own sake, to save her further embarrassment,' he said, 'all that is left to us is to consider what further comforts—not Excitements or Diversions—for example, cards would be too much—but rather how we might keep her softly enough that she does not grow agitated, but not so softly that she grows Fat. I shall outfit her new quarters precisely as we may decide is best for her, in consultation with Dr Hughes. I shall spare no expense, of course—however, we must look not to Indulgence and Fashion as our guide, but rather to howsoever we might best encourage a recovery based upon Scientific principles.' He spoke with his usual precision, low and certain. 'None shall fault me,' he added.

Freddie, my eldest brother, was in some agitation himself. His brow was quite furrowed, and his face was as grey as Father's. There had always been a great Indian carpet upon the library floor, woven in silk and wool of reds and yellows, which had faded and coalesced over the years to a respectable blood colour. Freddie's foot had found the corner nearest the hearth, and he was nervously turning it over with his toe, and back, and over, and back. It was testament to the depth of his feeling that he ventured to speak out against Father at all, for this was a domestic trespass we had learnt well, even as little children, that we must not commit. 'I do not know that we are in complete agreement, Father,' he said, with a tentativeness quite moving to see in one usually so assured. 'Would not it be kinder if she were to take an extended Holiday? I shall go with her—to Switzerland, perhaps, for the air—'

'We are all in perfect agreement,' said Father again, musingly, slowly, still looking at the clouds. An uncertain silence ensued, broken only by the rustling of the carpet under Freddie's foot as he persisted in pushing it back and forth.

'Stop that,' said Father, and Freddie at once became still. 'I have often thought we ought to replace that carpet,' Father went on. 'It is from my grandfather's time, and rather past its best.'

'Perhaps Mamma might enjoy use of it, and find comfort in its old Familiarity, in the attic,' said my middle brother, John. John and I were like Father in form, tall and thin, although John had a sportiness about him that I lacked. He would turn brown as a berry in the summer and go striding about the place. It was he who had the appearance and style of the first son, and he was indeed often taken as such by those making our acquaintance for the first time. There was a masterfulness in everything John did, from the imperious way he directed the servants, to the casual way he treated the ancient fixtures and furnishings of the house. Freddie, who would take the title upon Father's death, was much more like Mamma. He was a smaller person, quick-witted, but prone to melancholy.

I felt a sickness that had its origins in some abstract part of me, like the Soul, or similar. Freddie and I dared a discreet exchange of troubled glances between us.

I asked, 'How long, Doctor, do you think she might need to be so—' I could not go on, for the word that came to my mind was *imprisoned*, and I knew Father would not welcome that.

'Retired,' said John.

'Why, for as long as is necessary,' said the Doctor. 'Until such time that she is no longer in any danger.'

Danger?

Dr Hughes rippled obsequiously and began to discourse upon the general matter of Mamma. He had seen Bedlam, he said, and it was no place for a lady. 'Would you have her cast amongst the Drunk and Derelict? No!—Sir Alfred has said it well—it is for dear Lady Fox's own sake. Would you not rather to keep her close, where you might kindly watch her, and where I might attend her as often as is required?' He expounded upon this matter, offering some elaboration of his professional diagnosis of Mamma's distracted wits, and the perils of excessive Freedom, until my father, with a stately nod, caused him to dwindle to an awkward close.

'But, surely, our choices are not limited to, one, Bedlam, and two, the attic?' ventured Freddie.

Nobody responded to this remark.

Into the silence, I asked, 'How often might we visit her?'

'Perhaps once daily?' said the Doctor, looking at Father. Father inclined his head.

'We might try diurnal visits, and, between us, observe how she responds to so frequent attention. It may be it is too much.'

John was nodding sombrely. 'This is a sore blow for the family,' he said.

'Indeed. It is a great pity her scene was so thoroughly witnessed,' said Father. 'And we shall see what wide-ranging fruit your mother's trouble will engender. It shall not harm your prospects, Alfred, but I should not be amazed if you younger two find certain families once open to matrimonial arrangement, for example, are no longer quite such friends to us.'

'We had not so many guests yesterday,' said John.

'And yet people talk,' Father said, with a supercilious look that communicated what he thought of People.

'Shall we take meals with her?' asked Freddie.

'What—in the attic?' said John.

'Quietness is the key, here,' said the Doctor. 'Quietness—and Simplicity.'

'Indeed,' said Father. 'Like the holy Anchoress of old. Through prayer, and reflection, we may yet heal her Disturbed Mind.'

Freddie and I glanced quietly at one another again.

'Father—' I began, my sickness rising, when Wilson's entrance relieved me of the obligation of speaking. I felt awash with relief. Freddie looked at me once more, but now I did not return his glance. Wilson had bowed to my father, and then to us all, and finally, acknowledged me alone.

'Mr Gabriel,' he said. 'A note.' He presented me this communication upon his little silver salver.

'From whom?' asked Father.

'It is indicated that the sender is Mrs Prendergast, Sir Alfred,' said Wilson.

'I will take it,' said Father—and he did. 'Wait, for we may have a response,' he added to Wilson, who immediately turned invisible without leaving us, in the manner peculiar to good servants.

I did not know if my father was aware I had proposed to Susannah; Freddie knew, but would not betray me. I could but hope that John had not witnessed it, nor heard of it from some domestic Spy. As Father had said—People Talk.

'What business does the Prendergast relic have with you?' Father asked, unfolding the paper and peering down at it.

'I do not know,' I said, still carefully avoiding Freddie's eye.

'I cannot read this,' said Father. 'Where is my quizzing-glass?' When we were silent, he said, 'Well?'

'I am sure we do not know, Father,' said Freddie. 'Shall we send for Adley?'

'No—no. Read it,' he said, passing my note to Freddie.

Freddie looked at it.

'It is brief, Gabriel,' he told me. 'Mrs Prendergast asks that you attend her at home at your earliest convenience, even outside of the usual visiting-hours.'

'How singular,' said Father, looking at me. 'Why?'

I could not speak; I felt my cheeks aflame, and there was a ringing in my ears.

'The lady does not indicate the reason for this visit,' said Freddie, with a gentle voice.

'When was this delivered?' Father asked Wilson.

'Moments before I brought it here, Sir Alfred.'

'Prendergast has a ward, yes?' said Father. 'The girl. Comely, if one can look past the nose.'

Father knew perfectly well Susannah was Mrs Prendergast's ward; they were our nearest neighbours, and, what is more, Susannah had formed a close friendship with our cousin Charlotte, who was quite often with us. I do not know that he had ever spoken to her directly, but she had oft enough been our guest, and indeed we Mrs Prendergast's. And I am sure I do not need to say that there was nothing at all objectionable about her nose.

'Yes, Father,' said I.

'Susannah,' said Freddie.

'What is her parentage?'

'Well, sir, Mr Prendergast holds office in Burma, and her mother has gone to her reward.'

'Who was she?' Father asked.

'Miss Prendergast's mother? I do not know who she was.'

'Hmph. Money?'

I paled with silent indignation. 'I do not know,' I said, and did not add what welled in my heart, which was that I certainly did not care if she came with a King's Ransom, or nothing at all.

'Well, the old woman is well enough off, given that garish pile of hers. I suppose there will be provision for the girl. You are not intending to swoon, are you, son?'

I mumbled as deferentially as I could that a faint was not my intention.

'You had better go,' said Father. 'See what Prendergast wants of you.'

Before John had said it, I had already thought to suggest we put down a carpet—not the Indian carpet, if Father chose to remove it, but something soft in duck-egg blue and white—and also, perhaps give Mamma a book-shelf, and a good Feather-bed, and perhaps to have the chimney of the old fire up there well swept, to ensure her comfort in the attic, and perhaps not be too simple about her meals, but rather give her the things most agreeable to her. Not Linzer torte, as it had become political, but marrow toast, cutlets, roasted quail, jugged hare, apple dumplings, and whatever else she should like. And to allow her any such Visitors as might wish to see her, outside our own intimate circle, and to retain her lady's maid. And to make a case for daily turns about the winter garden.

Later—this I would do later.

As I made my exit, Father remarked to my brothers and the Doctor, 'She was not a bad woman. I can only be glad that she bore me sons.'

At the station, I spent the evening eating I know not what, for I cannot remember, and drinking rum, and I moved from a state of extreme hunger and drunkenness to satiation and sobriety, to hunger once again and a singularly buoyant sensation of neither drunkenness nor sobriety, but something beyond either. It passed my mind that I had nothing to offer in exchange for my food, whatever it may have been, and drink, but it also occurred to me that I had assisted in bringing the whale down, and that perhaps gave me licence to partake.

The Creature was a full fifty feet, and night had long fallen when Stockworth and his men finally brought it in. More than one man called it a Murderous Beast, and worse, but, although I did not say it, I felt it could hardly be blamed for defending itself from our violent incursion into its own Home.

The station was aflame with many lights in the dark and the black waves crested with white. Tam could not contain himself, and he leapt about in the freezing water. All hands were compelled to assist in heaving the beast ashore tail-first, but most hands were, like myself, profoundly drunk, and it was a slow and clumsy process. I stood amongst the men and pretended to heave, and the great corpse crept up the beach, and up, and up, until it was quite clear of the water, and we ceased our labour.

Heron went about quite red for a while, then shut himself in the stone house with Mrs Heron and the old woman.

Jack was so helpless to the rum's effects that he was struggling against the movements of his own face when he stumbled to roll himself weirdly upon the tail of the beast.

'The irons, Mr Fox! Those ridiculous-looking Contraptions from Timbuktu brought her down!' he cried.

'They are from America,' I said. 'Jack, please do excuse me—'

'I will purchase them from you,' he said. 'They are Marvels of Modern Technology.'

'Jack—please, will you take them as a gift? I have no wish to profit from them.' I felt quite ill whenever I thought of them, now, and longed only to be perfectly free of them. Only imagine strolling along, shoulders unburdened by jagged metal! Only imagine being free of their distraction!—although, I thought, I should have to find some other loud item that would keep the flesh-eating birds away—a hand-held bell might suffice. There was no place in my life for harpoons.

Jack stared at me with tears spilling from his drunken eyes. 'I wish you had been here, Mr Fox, in the great seasons, when the sea was thick with fish of every kind and, if you wanted one, you only had to poke the waves with a sharp stick and see what you brought up. Why, the sea was more fish than water! One could step Christ-like from fish to fish across the tops of the waves! True!'

'Sir, I thank you for your thoughts, which I believe you have already touched upon, earlier to-day. But really I must withdraw, for I am tired—'

'Men laboured hot from the oil-fires and were cooled only by the sweat of exertion. Elsewhere upon the island autumn iced over into winter, I am sure, but the station was consumed! Consumed by a Tropical Heat! I remember whole years of my childhood here slipping by in one continual summer of plenty, the station its own little world of fire suspended amongst snowy hills and brittle forests and the sea, which is quite cold, you know!' he told me, with an earnestness almost distressing to see.

I assured him I understood quite well that the sea was cold.

'Yes!—you were in there to-day with me. I had forgotten. Forgive me. But! Three chains of shore, two hot acres. Mr Fox! Hark! It was a good place, and it may yet be a good place. Please—please. When I turned fourteen it snowed in a perfect circle outside the buildings. True! In the slab huts we slept with the windows open and warm air breezing in and icicles twinkling in the trees beyond. Another time hail like fists tore through the branches and into the sea and we stood in the middle of it bareheaded under a clear blue sky and a gleaming Sun like God's great eye too glorious to behold blinking down at us. One year the storm that shifted boulders and hurled trees raged while we sat about and drank rum and dear old Mary who has been Ancient Forever hung—hanged?—hung?—pegged the laundry to dry on lines strung between the huts, remarking that we would benefit from a touch of the breeze, while behind her the very cliff-face trembled!'

'Jack—' I said. This great speech was causing in me an apprehension which began in my gut and thence advanced into my empty pockets—for how many times should somebody try to convince me to buy the station? I feared I might become worn down with the constant selling, and finally acquiesce. And then what should I do!

'In those days we hauled the marvellous Carcases end upon end from the sea. Like to-day! Like to-day, but every day—only nobody died. When I close my eyes, I can still see the lovely red wounds in a million different whales. A Hundred Million! And the ship! This was not long after my father had died, surely. The *Tristessa* was a beauty, Mr Fox! She was bought by a man called—well, I do not remember his name. But she operates out of Hobart-town now. I have seen her. When we had her, I would stare at the horizon and all at once she would—appear—from no-where!—appear before my eyes, huge-sailed, full-bellied, sinking under the weight of her Cargo! What a ship! Even to-day, I feel an echo of the thrill of rowing to meet her to disgorge her and tow her Cargo ashore. My lips, which to-day are soft, in those days cracked and bled with salt and wind. My hands were raw and oozing from the work! No—that is wrong. They are raw and oozing to-day, for I am now unaccustomed. In those days, although I was a boy, they were hard and horned like the thickest leather! We had dozens of station-hands and deck-hands—dozens upon dozens upon dozens of them, all getting rich, or, anyway, less poor, and speaking what must surely have been every language known to man. And there were the trading-days! Remember?'

Here I had to remind him that I had not been with him in those days.

'Of course you were not. You do not remember, but I do. The people! They were tall—they had a name—I do not remember it—they would come. What do you remember of them, Byrne?' he asked, for that man had approached us from the great cooking-fire upon the beach, and stood listening to Jack's ravings with a fired clay cup in his hand. 'What were they called?'

'I cannot say,' Byrne said.

'Well! They would come flickering amongst the forest of meaty flowers, half-rotten—but there were never flowers, why have I thought of that?—Mr Fox?—they would come, cloaked and painted with their hair in ropes, and their women shaven-headed and bare-breasted, from the slender grey trees, or along the sand, from the cold outside into the hot centre of the Earth with skins and game and vegetables to trade for whale-flesh and barrels of oil and whatever tea and sugar and flour we could spare, which was never enough, and I remember the cooking-fires burning as the red sun pooled on the sea horizon—which cannot be correct, for the sea horizon here is in the east—am I recalling a sun-rise?—at any rate, as night fell, their fires and our fires burnt in neighbourly fashion, or neighbourly enough, and the bounty of kangaroo steamer and damper and whale-meat and shellfish and rum and all the other things we had that were good, I cannot even remember them all now, passed from hand to hand into the night. I remember blue lights in the waves, dancing like nothing else—does anyone remember those?—blue sparks from an undersea fire, maybe. It sounds like Lunacy, but I know it is true! And green Ribbons of Light in the sky! I remember walking along the wet sand with the lights blossoming about my feet with every step! And the green above! In company! Other children with me saw it too and we ran and splashed each other with night waves full of—full of—light. Listen. This is important. There was a wall in the air, an invisible—what is the word? A *membrane*, dividing the station from the rest of the world. One could push through and be in the frozen wilderness outside. How my breath would hang white and the thrill of the cold would push under my fingernails until my hands went numb and it would freeze the juice in my eyes and shrivel my balls—excuse me for mentioning them—and punch down my throat to the very bottoms of my lungs! But there were ways to stay warm outside the circles of firelight! Boys and girls my own age running off with me into the forest to play. I remember becoming invisible when branches closed over the moon.

'I was a boy then. As a man I have never known such excess. Try to talk about it with anyone but the old woman Mary and they tell me they do not remember, or that it was never thus.'

'It was never thus,' said the old O'Riordan, beside me.

'Jack makes use of some poetic language,' I said.

'He practises,' said the old man.

'Yes, he stalks about the place with his lips moving,' said Byrne. 'Cook owed you a holey dollar,' he added to Jack, coming to put a superstitious hand upon the whale's flank. He shuddered.

'I did not take his bet,' slurred Jack.

'Go to bed,' said Byrne.

'Yes,' said Jack, and laid himself down upon the sand, and shut his eyes. 'When my father died, he let out a little sigh and crumpled like paper. And his skin crawled and tightened and drew his lips open so his false teeth popped out. It is a memory from very long ago, and I do not know how true it is.'

'Memory is a frail thing,' said Byrne softly.

'Would you like us to help you to your bed?' I asked Jack.

As seemed to occur for every second question I asked in that place, no one took the trouble to answer me, and I was left alone, as I had wished to be, but did not want, when the reality of it came upon me.

'You live too much for the past,' said Byrne to Jack—rough Byrne, with a voice so gentle! 'And too much in your head. Things were not better then. And things will not be better to-morrow. I can tell you what the future will be. The future will be troubled, because Life is troubled. Look with clear eyes at this rosy past you describe to me and you will see it was then just as it is now and will be.'

You are sorely in need of a making

HOLD A PICTURE IN YOUR mind of an enormous obsidian obelisk blocking out the sun, erected a thousand years ago by a Tyrant to commemorate his own might. Weathered but not beaten, it is plated in a highly conductive metal that attracts an extraordinary quantity of lightning-strikes every year, which further blacken it, and imbue it with a fierce and fiery charge. It casts a long shadow like a spear, which points directly towards your quaking coward's Heart. Conjure this dreadful image, and you will have some idea of the qualities of Mrs Prendergast. She was at least a thousand years old, and garbed in black with black veil, and her bent fingers were spiked with bright sharp rings, and she carried a gold-topped cane, and in every other way she was exactly the obelisk I have described, in the form of a human.

Despite the growing night and the freezing air, I elected to take Pharaoh and go across the fields to the obelisk, rather than to travel by road in the greater comfort of the pony and trap (or, most comfortable of all, to be driven in the landaulette). Comfort is a Danger! It makes one soft. My perturbation of spirit was such that I welcomed the cold whip of the air. Mamma had always said that a bracing breath of fresh air was all one ever needed to knock sense into one. Many a time we had gone out together, afoot, charging up hill and down dale, to cure our diverse sadnesses.

As Pharaoh's hoof-beats pounded through the fields of my childhood, I made a cheering story for myself. Susannah had confessed to Mrs Prendergast that I had proposed, and told her that she (Susannah) had been so astonished that she had refused me, when truly she had meant to accept, and that she would like Mrs Prendergast's guidance on how she might correct her mistake. And, my story went, Mrs Prendergast was indeed appalled at my poor timing, and that I had not first spoken to her of the matter. But, ultimately, she was warmed by the understanding of my honest heart, and my sincere love for Susannah, and had thus summoned me to, First, chide me, and Second, give me the girl. She would say something like, 'Long have I considered that you would make her a good match, for though your father is a hard man, you have turned out differently. But you must promise to take care of her.' And I would press Susannah's hand to my bosom and make that promise, and Susannah would do or say something dear and modest.

The black ground sped beneath Pharaoh's great hooves, and the old trees bent and whispered. I passed from field to field, losing my courage at every gate to make the leap, instead halting Pharaoh, and dismounting, and opening the gate, and leading him through, and closing the gate, and remounting, very unlike the dashing Suitor. I was glad Father was not there to witness my timidity. At the last, however, I came to the low dry-stone wall bordering the final stretch of road to the Prendergast house. I could turn away, and ride for some distance from my destination, and go through another gate there—or I could charge boldly on and leap the wall! Without permitting myself time to grow afraid, I urged Pharaoh forth, moved my hands to his neck, and made the jump. I felt my Belly lurch, and my hat whip from my head, and the dreadful crunch as Pharaoh's hoof clipped the wall. We landed clumsily, but intact. I drew him up and saw the half-broken stones, and my hat beyond, and thought that perhaps the story with which I had comforted myself was not true.

There was an intimate extravagance in the pink and gold of the sunrise, unrolling its glow over the sea horizon, and melting into a day as bright and cold as diamond. The waves pushed against our oars. We were alive, all but one, skating along the earth's midline, tiny between the giddy depths below and above. A black lump drifted ahead, far littler than the whale. At first I thought it some arrangement of dead branches, but as we drew near it floundered awake and disappeared beneath the surface. 'Seal,' said my Cannibal—William.

Mrs Heron and Mary sat together in the very bow of the boat, and therefore I could not see them as I rowed, and yet I heard their soft voices from time to time.

The men and I would row a straight south-westerly course, in favourable wind, keeping the coast starboard, and rowing and rowing, and allowing the sun to stain the sky from below the sea up and over our heads at its zenith and dip again down behind Mount Wellington and the spires of Hobart-town. That is what I was told, and I accepted it with the dumb resignation I had learnt from dear Tigris. Poor Tigris! She which I had bought with Mrs Prendergast's money!

The shadow of the obelisk stretched like a dagger right into my heart.

Perhaps that is a touch melodramatic.

I went like a little leaf in the water, pulled along by the current, letting an oar be put once more in my hands. This, although I thought I might vomit yet more at the mere thought of going out upon the sea again, and at the prospect of sitting all day in the company of the soft and dripping Cook, lashed down the middle of the benches, whom I had neither killed nor saved. God, whosoever You are, grant me return to the enclosed fields of England! Let me dwell once more where there is no Sea in sight, and my troubles are no greater than bulls getting shot, and a soul-deep shame about my mother's treatment, and a father who does not like me, and a girl who will not love me!

Although the way I had taken across the fields was quicker than the road, my stopping and starting had caused such delay it was quite dark when finally I gave Pharaoh to a groom and was allowed entrée within the Prendergast house. Pots of fragrant sage were either side of the carven door, and I pulled a leaf and rolled it between my fingers before I stepped within.

Mrs Prendergast's house was not ancestral, I fear. Father's exception to the elderly lady was never that she was an obsidian obelisk, crackling with lightning. That he did not mind. What he did mind was that Mrs Prendergast had inherited an astonishing quantity money he thought she did not deserve from a benefactress, a titled Irish lady to whom Mrs Prendergast had been Companion in her younger years. She had thus been elevated all at once from a position rather lowlier. Her house was nicely made, I had always thought, very modern, with a ballroom larger and brighter than our own, and charming gardens, and sufficient appointments for the full complement of servants.

The brisk manservant who had opened the door to me bade me tidy myself, right there in the hall. He took away my coat and hat (which I had retrieved whence it had flown from my head in the field) and pulled off his own gloves to bat away the dust from the place where I sit down. Tutting, he removed the bruised sage-leaf from my gloved hand, and then deprived me of the gloves themselves, as they were coarse riding-gloves. I did not know on whose authority he treated me so archly! The scent of crushed sage touched the air about us. At last, when I was brushed, stripped and beaten to his satisfaction, he permitted himself to conduct me into his employer's presence.

'Is Miss Prendergast in attendance of Mrs Prendergast?' I quietly asked the man.

'I am afraid I do not know, sir,' he lied, with a short and dismissive bow.

Mrs Prendergast was solitary in the drawing-room, arranged upon a green settee before the fire. Her black dress was draped dramatically against the velvet. A ridiculous will-o'-the-wisp of a dog lay snoring upon a red cushion at her feet. The lady held a leather-bound Bible, but she was not reading it, for it was closed. This Book bore an elaborate golden Crucifix stamped upon the cover. Her spectacles, also golden, were folded upon the arm of the settee.

She looked up when the manservant announced me, saying, 'Ah, good,' and waving me forwards. Thus was I drawn into the presence of the obelisk, who was rather less obelisk-like when horizontal, and indeed rather small. She was possessed of a strong chin and nose, but there was a softness about her I do not know that I had ever seen before. Her hair looked like a dollop of good cream in the firelight.

'Sit there, Mr Fox,' she said, pointing a knobbly finger at a low red chair to one side of the hearth, whose cushion, I silently observed, had been given to the dog.

Mrs Prendergast was an Irishwoman, although she had resided in England as our Neighbour for as long as I could remember. Her dark eyes were grown milky, and her cheek sunken, but there was a quickness about her, and a sharpness, and a hint of wry humour. She had the perfect teeth of the old—that is, they were false.

'Madam,' I said. 'I am honoured to attend you, and hope I find you well.'

'Thank you, Mr Fox; my health is perfect,' she said.

'And long may it continue so,' said I. 'It is quite cold outside,' I went on. After all, if I were speaking, she could not give me bad news. 'The talk is that it will snow in the morning.'

'Are you complaining about the ride over here?'

'No! Madam—it is my honour and my pleasure. I am merely making conversation.'

'Yes, we shall have a conversation, and not about the weather, either. Susannah is in quite a state, you know.'

A flare of gorgeous hope! 'I am most deeply sorry if I have caused the young lady any dismay,' I said, the warmth of satisfaction in my heart. 'I take it she may have spoken to you about the matter that passed between us?'

'"The matter that passed between us"—what a peculiar turn of phrase. Do not be so coy, Mr Fox,' said the old lady. 'Did you imagine that she would not confide in me? Of course she did, for I am her guardian and her confidante. You proposed to her, and she refused you, and this upon the very afternoon your poor mother was so taken ill.'

'Indeed, madam, my timing was very ill-chosen, but I was driven by such ardent admiration and deep affection—'

'Oh, do stop,' she said. 'I have no interest in the confessions of a young man's heart. Susannah is upset, for she was very troubled by your poor mother's turn. She is possessed of a tender heart and strong natural sympathies, and she was quite alarmed at how no one of your family rushed to the Lady's aid, or went after her, when she withdrew from the room. Indeed, I could see that she was undertaking to go herself, until I stopped her with a Look. And she was naturally troubled anew by your proposal, which, she said, shows that you were thinking only of yourself at the moment that your mother sorely needed a friend.'

I leapt to my feet. 'Madam, no!' I cried. 'I was thinking of—' But I could not honestly conclude my remark, for I supposed I had indeed been thinking of myself. 'Madam, with all my deepest respect for you and for Miss Prendergast, perhaps I might be permitted to say, humbly, that knowing Mamma as I did, indeed do, I felt at that time that she would wish for a moment alone.'

'No, one or the other of you ought to have gone with her. Sit down, Mr Fox,' she said dryly. 'I find myself in danger of chastising you, and that is not my wish. Indeed, this is not at all the matter I wish to discuss with you now.'

'It is not?' I said, sitting meekly.

'I watch the people about me, my boy,' she said. 'I have observed you as you have grown from a white and weedy boy into a white and weedy young man. Like a little sapling trying to thrive in the shadow and root-system of an enormous Oak.' She did not speak cruelly, although her words were not pleasant to hear. Rather, she spoke as though she were referencing that which was commonly understood.

Nevertheless, I could not speak at once. White and weedy!

'I do not blame you, you know. It is a difficult thing, to have the father you have had.'

'Madam,' I said. 'I thank you for the charming frankness of your words . . .'

'Oh, do not talk to *me* about charming frankness, Gabriel Fox,' she said. 'I was born in the previous century, which was a different time, and have now lived long enough—and have acquired enough money—that I have earnt the right to speak as naturally as I please, without much care for Convention, which is, in fact, a Suffocating Net that keeps us low, and away from one another.'

I made to say something more, but she held up a hand, and I fell silent.

'Neighbour, I have a task for you,' she went on, 'and I urge you with every fibre of my Being to accept, for it may be the making of you. And you are sorely in need of a making!'

The old lady began the great task of rearranging her person, and I arose to assist her, hovering in a very ungainly way.

'Sit down,' she told me. 'You are an exceedingly anxious young man, aren't you? Forever leaping to your feet.'

'I hoped only to assist you, madam,' I said, resuming my seat, and resolving to remain there, come hellfire.

'Assist me? In sitting more comfortably? I am not quite so far gone as that,' she said, calm and a little amused. 'You have not enquired about the task I have mentioned, which tells me you are not over-eager to have it,' she continued. 'But have it you shall.' And now she opened the Bible upon her lap to remove two small paper packets tucked within. 'This is a letter of credit,' she said, passing the first to me. 'And this is a personal letter,' she told me, giving me the second, which was considerably more substantial than the first. 'I charge you to deliver this letter on my behalf, Mr Fox. It must be delivered by hand, for I do not have an address.' She sighed, and closed her book, and stroked its cover absent-mindedly. She wore a large Ruby upon her right hand, and it glimmered as she moved. 'Your mother has made me think of this,' she said, 'though it has long been my intention to send my letter. I wrote it many years ago. Lady Fox's words yesterday—her pure and simple expression of Unhappiness—now *there* was what you call charming frankness—did flare a little light on the circumstances of my own heart.'

Was Mrs Prendergast confessing to me that she was Unhappy? The prospect seemed so unlikely it was almost comical. This not only because the lady had ever radiated a deeply self-satisfied contentment from the very core of her being, but also that she clearly did not think terribly highly of me, and surely would not bother confiding in me. I turned the packets she had given me over in my hands. The one Mrs Prendergast had told me contained the letter of credit was unmarked, but the other, the personal letter, was inscribed with a name.

'Maryanne Maginn,' I read aloud.

'Maryanne,' said Mrs Prendergast. Any trace of comedy was gone as she pronounced the name. 'She has long been lost to me, and I would have her back.'

That morning in the hut, I had prised open my sore and crusted eyes, beheld my clothing of the day before in a sodden lump upon the floor, and rolled forth to untangle two masses of paper from the jacket. The first mass was my letter of credit, and the second was the letter Mrs Prendergast had written for her long-lost Maryanne Maginn. Even my reflections upon the importance of Letters upon the beach with Mrs Heron and her Balloon had not inspired me to remember these vital epistles, abandoned to wet ruin in the clothing I had torn from my cold and hurting body upon our return from the disastrous hunt.

From his comfortable repose in a bunk near mine, William asked me why I was on the floor, and in despair. The more I tried to salvage the papers, which were still dripping with sea water, the more torn and lumpish they became, and the more the ink flowered and bled, until, ultimately, I was left with nothing but a soggy grey mass in either hand, representing all the money I had in the world, and all the substance of my Purpose there.

'Now you are Truly Free,' William said.

'I hope you will forgive me for remarking that your observation is most profoundly unhelpful, William.'

'I forgive you. Besides—perhaps it is untrue, and you are not Free at all. Do you know that the Chinese believe that if a man saves your life, you belong to that man? Or perhaps it is the other way around. I do not recall.'

'Of course I do not know that,' I said. 'And we are not Chinese.'

'No, indeed.'

'I am grateful that you saved me.'

'You say the words, but you do not seem particularly glad to have life.'

'I suppose in this moment I am not, but I am sure it will pass.'

'Go and pay a visit to Cook, and he will make you glad to be alive. Anyway—are you not selling your irons to Jack? You might make a little money thus, which will be enough to get you on your way.'

'I made a gift of them to him.'

'What! After all our walking! Why?'

'I wished to be rid of them.'

'You would have been rid of them had you sold them.'

'Yes, I know.' I paused, and got up off the earthen floor. 'Perhaps he will let me have these clothes in payment for them,' I said, for not only were my own things still almost as wet as they had been while actively in the sea, but they were crusted and clogged with salt and sand, and would require a thorough laundering. The only good thing to come of my own dousing was that my handkerchief, which had remained filthy and folded in my pocket, was perfectly clean once more, with my mother's clever embroidery shining a clear green against the white.

How could I return to Hobart-town, and take up once more my Purpose, without my letters? I had no money! And no proof of she whom I represented.

'Do you know of a farmer called McNamara?' I asked William.

'Oh, yes, he is a landholder of some note west of here,' said he. 'Cattle, I believe.'

'I have heard he is seeking labourers,' I said.

'Where would you have heard that?' he asked.

'Oh—at the Royal Hotel.'

'I worked for McNamara,' said Byrne, who had been snoring mere moments before. 'As a Free man. Pendle worked for him as an assigned man. I would not go there again.'

'Beggars should not be choosers,' I said.

'You are not a beggar,' said William.

'I may be, now.'

'The work is very hard,' Byrne told me.

'I am a farmer's son,' I said. 'I am entirely capable of hard work.'

'Are you, truly?' asked William, propping himself upon one arm, and squinting, for the air was gelatinous with night-farts. 'When you say you are a farmer's son, do you not mean you are the son of some squire, who lives in a big house, and has land that is farmed for him by an army of men?'

'I work with the men in the summers,' I said, with some indignation. There was general laughter; more men than I had previously thought were awake and listening to our exchange.

'No, you would not manage at McNamara's,' said Pendle, from some dark corner somewhere. 'Come back south to Hobart-town when we take Cook to-day.'

'Yes,' said Jack. 'I will introduce you to my mother.'

'I had thought you slept outside, Jack!' said Byrne.

'It was too cold. And the whale gave me Nightmares. Keep the clothing, Mr Fox,' he said to me, sitting up to plant his feet upon the floor and rub his face with his hands. And the men began musing amongst themselves about two of their number who had slipped into the trees together in the night, in order to embrace. I found this comforting, in fact: my troubles were so little and unremarkable to them that they could fluidly move the discussion to other topics, and not thrash and wail in despair at the hopelessness of my situation.

That comfort did not last long, slipping from me as I exited the hut in the pre-dawn dark, for I was too occupied with the cold to allow myself to indulge any such warming sensation as that.

My beliefs do not control the Universe

I HAD SAID BUT LITTLE since we had departed the station. The men about me spoke from time to time, but the overwhelming mood was grave, and their pronouncements were brief, and spoken in low voices. The corpse of Mr Cook loomed very large. I was occupied internally, giving myself some hard words over and over, chastising myself again and again for my own foolishness and distraction, which had led me so far from Maryanne Maginn, and thus Susannah. What would I do without money? I should have to find work of some kind, and try to raise enough funds for my passage Home, and there face down Mrs Prendergast, and my own failure, and my eternal Loneliness, and consider what to do next.

No! I could not think of it. I must indeed find work, and for the first time in my life make some money. Then I must divert all my energies to the securing of Maryanne Maginn, and let no Distraction come upon me. And were she dead, I would bring her back to life, and carry her on my back to Norfolk, and throw her at Susannah's feet.

We would occasionally pass a hamlet or a house on shore, or a drift of smoke suggestive of human life beyond the trees. These settlements were quiet, although there were people and animals here and there. Women mending nets mouthed words below the breeze and water. A dog barked; a seabird called. A man shouted and a woman called a reply. Cows raised their heads to watch the boat skate by. A boy Tam's age stood knee-deep in the water, grey-skinned with cold, watching us. Tam had wanted to go with us. He was afraid, he had said. They had told him he would only be in the way. The coast undulated, sweeping wide and then narrow, rearing high into rocky cliffs, and dipping low again, rustling with papery trees. Great pools of sunshine moved across the land. I fancied I saw my own family's house, that great and ancient Hall, perched upon a rocky clifftop—but of course it was not there. The only structures on so grand a scale upon that Isle were not built by men but were entirely natural, like mountains, and whales.

The problem in the lamplight of the morning had been where to stow Cook in his shroud. In the bilge was not correct, although most convenient, and, anyway, Mrs Heron's and Mary's bags—though they had brought little, a carpet-bag for Mrs Heron and an old leathern pouch for Mary—were stowed there, wrapped in oilskin in order to keep them dry. My own clothes, damp still from my time in the sea, were bundled there, too, tied with string. There was some decking aft and stern on all the whaleboats, enough for a corpse, but this had also seemed incorrect, for the men had tried it, while I watched, for I had given up all facility of my own. They stood back to survey their work, and saw that they had made of Cook a dreadful figurehead. And that is why they had finally lashed him betwixt us all. Thus, as I rowed, my elbow nudged him again and again, and although I perceived that the shroud was dry, I slowly developed the sensation that his body was yet soaked with sea water, and this wetness seeped into my jacket and onto my skin that way, and I began to shiver all over my body, not from cold, but that I was clammy with water from the corpse.

No one had pissed over the side all morning. I suppose this was in deference to the presence of ladies, and perhaps the corpse. Before we had departed, it had been decided with Heron back at the station that we would row without stopping in order to make the best time, but either no one had considered, or no one had been bold enough to mention, the necessities of Nature. Therefore, when the sun was high above us, we very hastily pulled into a cosy bay and leapt out, dragged the boat upon the sand and helped the women down, and dispersed rapidly and apologetically into the trees.

When we convened once again, the tacit understanding was to pretend that we had pulled in for dinner. Mary had great handfuls of dry leaves, and some sticks under her arms, and without ceremony, she used a kind of magic unknown to me to spark a fire using no tool but her bare hands. 'Do we need a fire?' asked Mrs Heron. 'Surely we shall not stop long?'

'Need a cup of tea, of course,' said Mary. She had produced, from somewhere, a tin pot with a handle, and a packet of tea, a loaf of bread, and a large ceramic jar, stopped with cork, which she opened with a knobby hand. 'Mutton steamer,' she said.

'Mutton?' I asked.

'Kangaroo,' said William. 'All meat is mutton to good Mary.'

'And, in fact, not kangaroo, but wallaby,' said the Scotsman.

'I need water, for the tea,' said Mary, and William courteously arose to retrieve the cask from the boat.

Mary kindly scooped a great mound of pink and gelid meat onto a piece of bread. This was a troubling repast, in the visual sense, but I accepted it like any ruffian, with both hands. We used to eat jugged hare sometimes in the summer, when the groundsman's boys would set snares and bring us their catch. When I was a very small child, my mother would take me to look at the traps, and I would cry, and she would comfort me, and we would think of names for the poor brown hares, like Flop-ear, and Trumpet, and, later, we would eat them, unsentimentally, smiling at one another with red fibres in our teeth. My mother loved to tell me the story of the man who died of eating hare.

After it had been so long promised, I could scarcely taste the Steamer—be it mutton or kangaroo or wallaby—all but sickened as I was by memory.

Mrs Heron did not eat, but instead rose from her place by the fire, and went and stood by the whaleboat—by Cook.

Before we had left, Heron had said: 'Do not take longer than you require.' I was free, but the others had assured him they would not. 'You might sleep in the boat,' he said, and the men said with all due respect they would stay in a place called Wapping, and Heron did not answer but nodded. There was some unspoken significance in this which I did not comprehend.

'You, Mr Fox—will you go with Mr Montserrat and my lady wife to the house of Mrs Montserrat?' he had asked me.

I could not remember if I had been told whether Mrs Montserrat was Jack's mother or his wife.

'Yes, he will,' said Jack, and Mr Heron put a hand on his breast and shot a private look upwards to God, presumably, as though I had just been Saved.

'Well done,' he said. 'Will you give the lady my warmest regards?'

'Yes,' said Jack.

I supposed Mr and Mrs Heron must have made their private farewell in the house, for they parted with placid warmth, as though they were friends who had passed a very nice visit together, and would see one another sometime soon, probably.

'Where is Tam?' asked Mrs Heron.

'I have not seen him, Leah,' said her husband gently.

Mrs Heron looked about her, gazing into the trees particularly. 'I had wished—' she began, and fell quiet, and then she said, 'Tell him God bless him.'

'I shall,' said Heron. 'Send your lady mother my regards,' said he to Jack, once more. 'Be so kind.' He had the look about him of a man who wished to say more.

'Yes, I will,' said Jack.

Gazing into the flames on that beach, halfway to Hobarttown, with the dead Cook moistly awaiting us to finish our tea and rum and kangaroo steamer, I was visited by a vision of Mr Heron as I had last seen him, his massive legs the last of him to fade from view as we rowed away. I stole a glance at Mrs Heron, and wondered if she had seen her husband for the last time.

'Shall we be off?' called Mrs Heron. The wind had risen, and it whipped her skirts.

I had grown generally warm by the fire, but my arm was still cold where it had nudged continually against Cook. 'I find I cannot help but disturb Cook with my elbow as I row,' I said, as we stamped upon the fire, and threw sand on it, and gathered together our few things. 'Does anybody else present find themselves continually brushing up against his shroud?'

The men looked at me. Along with my Cannibal William, present were Jack, and Byrne, and Pendle, and the tall Scot, whose name was McAvoy. 'No,' said William.

'But if you are, it does not matter,' said McAvoy as we were spilling down the sand to the whaleboat. 'He does not care.'

I did not feel I could say, But *I* care, for it troubles me very much.

Mrs Heron said something to me, but whatever it was, the wind picked it from her lips and threw it away.

When I left Mrs Prendergast, I found I could recall but little of our conversation—perhaps because there had been not much of substance to it, other than some practical directions regarding my voyage. The lady's knowledge of Maryanne Maginn and her circumstances was paltry enough, and she had, I think, kept some of what little she did know from me.

'She was a girl of fifteen,' she had said, at one juncture. 'Just a child. But she would remember me.'

I wished to confirm that which I dared hope: that if I were successful in the undertaking, Susannah should marry me, for I would have had my 'making', as the old lady had put it. And yet I did not speak this hope aloud, for it seemed fragile, and might break.

The snow, which I had thought would not fall until the morning, had begun to sigh down upon me as I made my weary way back across the fields and home. I was exhausted, bodily but also in my mind, by the interview with Mrs Prendergast. Nevertheless, I crept by the library, thinking I would re-join the conference if it yet continued and make my suggestion that Mamma be allowed book-shelves, and the other comforts I had thought of. I still wore my overcoat, gloves, and riding-boots. The dainty snowflakes caught upon these items had begun to melt. I left great wet footprints behind me, though I trod softly.

The library door was a little ajar, and I heard Father's voice. I hesitated. What should I tell him about my interview with Mrs Prendergast? How should he receive the news that I had agreed to leave all I knew within the month for Van Diemen's Land? As I paused there, wavering between entering and creeping away, I came to realise from the particularly furtive tone in which my father was speaking that my brothers were no longer ensconced within. I was privy to the conversation between Father and Dr Hughes, and none other.

'In the circumstances, a divorce would be widely understood, certainly amongst the more enlightened thinkers in your circle,' said Dr Hughes. 'It would free you to—'

'No, Hughes,' said Father. 'In her condition, surely, before long . . .'

Hughes inclined his head. 'I cannot imagine it will be so very long,' he said.

'Shall we have trouble from Customs, for bringing in a dead body?' I asked, as we recommenced our journey south, rowing in a leisurely manner.

'No, their reach is not so far,' said William. 'Not if you know where you might skirt it. There is a shipyard we know that does not give any trouble, and we shall make ground there, and go on foot without Cook, and ask his wife what she would have us do.'

'It is so easy?'

'Yes—this is a rustic place.'

'The poor woman,' said Mrs Heron, her eyes closed against the sun, even under her bonnet. 'I should like to go and comfort her.'

'She lives in Wapping, you know, madam,' said Jack.

'I have seen my share of poverty, and crime, and vice,' said Mrs Heron. 'And Cook was a good man—the honest poor live in Wapping, side by side with the fallen.'

'I met Mr Fox in Wapping,' said William, by way of conversation.

'No!' said I.

'Yes, the inn where I found you, the Cock and Bale, where you were talking so cosily with that young Woman, who was then ejected from the place for Sinfulness, is a famous place there, famously well-to-do, for there you might buy Wine, as well as rum and beer.'

'Why did you find him?' asked Byrne.

'What a question! He himself asked me something similar, on our journey down to the station—something about Fate, and the Why of things. I do not understand your question, Byrne,' said William.

'Your question is clear to me, and I have wondered it myself,' I told Byrne. 'Why did you engage with me, and take me on?' I asked William. 'Why did you put me in the way of Tigris? Why take me to the station?'

'Do you know of the Harmonic Method, sir?' he asked.

There were a few significant glances amongst the company in the boat.

'I do not.'

'Perhaps that is not surprising, as I am almost certain it is my own invention. I do not know—perhaps I read of it somewhere, or someone told me. I do not know. The Harmonic Method seeks to unite individuals, or individual groups, with shortcomings, or obstacles, or problems, which might be solved in a complementary fashion, by coming together in Harmonic Exchange. Our case is a fine example of this: you were in need of a horse, the German was in need of divesting himself of a horse, post haste, and I owed the German a debt, which was weighing upon me. Why can I not, I asked myself, Why can I not introduce the English gentleman to the German gentleman, that one might buy the horse from the other, and thus satisfy both needs, and meanwhile, if I have been of service to the German, and have assisted him out of his difficulty, will that not go some way towards forgiving me my debt? And so it was! Further: the station at which I was employed, managed by the good Mr Heron, was failing—excuse me for saying so—' This last remark was directed over his shoulder at Mrs Heron, who I could see only out of the very corner of my eye, framed in sunlight and not at all listening to our discussion. 'I thought: what is there to lose, but that I might introduce a new element to a place in decline, and put Jack in the way of some interesting new Technology, and perhaps improve our luck . . .' He trailed off, as the shrouded Cook sucked all the talk out of him.

'Harmonic Method!' Jack said, with a scoff. 'Sounds like Opportunism to me—or Communism, at best.'

'I do not know what Communism is,' said William.

'Neither does Jack,' said Byrne.

'Have there been other cases of this Harmonic Method of yours, sir, or was this your inaugural attempt?' I asked.

'By no means; indeed, I have put this method to use many a time, and always with great success. I once joined seven individuals thus. This was in Ireland. The seven people were my wife, our baby, a wet-nurse, the local squire, his daughter, a French tutor, and myself. I shall tell you of it some time.'

'And what did I receive, from our journey north?' I asked.

'What?'

'You call it an Exchange—what did I get in return for my contributions? For without my letter of credit, and the personal letter I carried, and my clothing, and all my goods that were stolen from me, I feel I am rather worse off than I was before I met you—materially, that is, for I am sure I am bettered for having met you otherwise,' I added politely.

'Are you? Well. Perhaps whatever is due you is still on its way to you,' he said. 'I do not know; I do not control Fate.'

'You told me the day before yesterday that you do not believe in Fate.'

'That does not mean it does not exist. My beliefs do not control the Universe, Gabriel Fox! What a strange suggestion you make!'

This was a great deal of information to take in. I paused and sorted through the many ideas he had presented before I said, 'You have a child?'

'I have two children,' said William. 'They are twins, as a matter of fact.'

'And they are back in Ireland, with one of your wives?'

'One of my wives!' he cried. 'What!'

Shame-facedly, I said, 'You told me that you had one or two wives.'

'Oh, for the love of God, you dear simple man,' he said. 'I was being glib.'

I stammered some foolish thing as he shook his head at Heaven. 'Never mind, never mind,' he told me. 'To answer your question: yes, my children are in Ireland, with my—one and only—wife, Mary O'Riordan.'

'Do they not miss you?' I asked.

'I should hope so,' he said.

I climbed the long and narrow servants' stair to the attic and found Freddie by the attic door, seated upon the hard boards. He was resting his head in his hands. I paused, for he looked quite unhappy, and I thought perhaps I ought to leave him alone. I felt for that moment that our positions were reversed; that I were the elder brother, and he the younger.

Freddie looked slowly up at me, and I could see the red of recent tears upon his face. I politely inspected the crossbeams of the rude ceiling, that we might both pretend I had not seen his emotion.

'You stayed very late with Mrs Prendergast. Is it terribly cold outside?' he asked me, his voice effortfully steady. His words fell flat into my ear-drums.

'Oh, rather,' I said. 'It has begun to snow.'

Freddie acknowledged this amiably and commenced a remark about how he had expected that the weather would continue clear to-night, and perhaps not snow until the morning, when he very abruptly stopped himself. There was a silence.

'It is quite a heavy fall,' I said helpfully. 'I think the roads will be quite covered by morning.'

'Stop that now,' he said, and then, with odd precision and hollowness to his words, he continued, 'We must be ... *sincere* with one another. It is difficult.'

'Yes,' I said, without seeking clarity from him if he thought the sincerity was difficult, or the situation in general, because I could apprehend that he meant both.

'I think she must be asleep. At least, she will not answer my knock,' he told me slowly, as though choosing and plucking each word like a berry from a bush.

'She must be weary indeed,' I said, in the same strange tone, lingering at the top of the stair. 'Dr Hughes has spoken at such length about how she must rest.'

'Dr Hughes is an old quack who cares nothing for Mamma and everything for Father's purse,' said Freddie, with more naturalness now. He sighed, and rested his head back against the wall behind him. 'And whatever glamour he feels will rub off on him from the family.'

'Oh, come now,' I said. 'That is not true. I will allow that he does have a touch of the sycophant about him, but that does not make him bad.'

'No, indeed; he is bad besides being sycophantic.'

'He was always very good with our various maladies—do not forget that he saved me from the Scarlet Fever.'

'He would have killed you, with his Fashionable methods, had we not engaged that good sensible Nurse to assist him, and discreetly undo all his work,' said Freddie.

'I do not remember a Nurse,' I said.

'She was there,' he told me. 'She was a Frenchwoman, so Father did not approve. You could not understand a word she said to you. Mamma engaged her. Do you truly not remember? Comtois was the name. Quite a small person.'

'No, indeed, I truly cannot remember.'

'Well, you were very ill, I suppose.'

I could not decide what would be best: to go away, or sit by Freddie, or remain standing. He was only a few feet from me, and yet he seemed far away, off in the distance. Indeed, I felt a curious remove from events as they were unfolding; from Mamma's plight, Father's cruelty, Freddie's distress, Susannah's rebuffal, and from my imminent journey. If I thought too deeply of any of these matters an affliction came over me, and so I allowed them to exist as they were and remained cautiously in their periphery.

Freddie saw my uncertainty. 'For God's sake, just come and sit by me,' said he. 'Are we not brothers?'

'Where is John?' I asked.

'Do we care?' he said.

When I slid down onto the creaking boards by him, we both faltered. Our conversation until this point had been uncharacteristically candid, and somehow, by drawing closer, and committing to the talk by seating myself with him, I had hurt this strange intimacy. We exchanged pained smiles. I reached up to the doorknob and tried it.

'You know it is locked, my dear Gabriel,' said Freddie.

'Why do we not call Mrs Tully?' I asked. Mrs Tully was the housekeeper, and would let us in.

'Father has taken her key,' he said. Dropping his voice, he went on with a new surge of emotion. 'Dr Hughes gave Father the advice that, because Mamma requires rest and seclusion, Father ought to exert full control of her situation, and her company, and, in short, collect all spare keys to this door. Only he might unlock it now. He—and Betty Sikes. *She* was deemed worthy,' he added, his pale cheeks flushing a deep red.

I could not immediately come up with an appropriate response to this. Finally, I said, 'What shall you do when he goes to London? How shall you get in?'

'Why, then we must rely on the good graces of Mrs Sikes.'

'She does not have any "good graces"!' I said.

'Gabriel—why did you say, "what shall *you* do"? Why not "we"?' he asked, as though he had only now truly heard my previous words. He shifted his position, so that he might look at me better. 'What did Mrs Prendergast want of you?'

I looked again into the ceiling-beams. Perhaps I might take a lesson from the servants. If I were still enough, and silent enough, he would forget I was there!

'I need your assistance in this matter,' he said. 'I do not wish to make this fight alone.'

But in every line of my body, and my every guilty breath, he read it: I would be gone within the month.

The most wretched wretch of all

I HAD SEEN HOBART-TOWN ONLY in the rain-slicked night, and then in the pre-dawn silence, with my head down and my harpoons over my shoulder. It had seemed an icy, impossible world, black, with oily lights in the distance.

It was afternoon as we finally rowed into the harbour in the whaleboat—late afternoon, when the shadows grow long, and workers begin to flock homewards. Hobart-town was grand on the large scale, and mean on the small. It was cupped between a great snowy-shouldered mountain and the slate-grey harbour, spilt at the bottom of wooded slopes, pooling its houses and streets in the little hollow afforded it by Nature, and setting its populace free to wander around and around. Well—Free is of course the wrong word. We skirted the flanks of the great

Ships in the harbour, and rounded a point to steal guiltily into a shipyard.

'Stay there, if you wish,' said McAvoy the Scotsman to me, as we drew close enough in that we might roll over the sides and heave the boat up the ramp and ashore.

Though I scarcely wished to jump into the freezing cold water again, I gritted my teeth and went in with the men and set my shoulder to the boat.

As I was handing Mrs Heron down from the boat to dry land, a man with the largest teeth I had ever seen on Man or Beast emerged from a low shed to greet us like his own brothers and sisters. This man was called Spire, it transpired, and was very congenial to accommodate our presence there, for a token fee. 'But,' he said, 'if you are discovered, I know you not at all.'

Then we divided our party, with some men and Mary remaining with Cook's body and the boat, and Mrs Heron, William, Jack and I setting off on foot to find Mrs Cook.

As we traipsed along the middle of the muddy streets, horse-shit and Urchins underfoot, the low buildings piled up upon one another as they need not be on that mostly empty Isle, the mountain blotting out the last of the sun's citric rays above, I thought how my mother had always said that all things look lovelier and more melancholy at night, and in the rain.

A forest of masts moved gently in the hidden swells and tides of the harbour, ropes and furled sails trembling like leaves and vines.

I reflected again upon the horrors of the voyage from England and was beset by a surge of worriment for Mrs Heron, especially poorly as she was, surrendering herself to such hardship.

'Should you not be afraid of the voyage Home, Mrs Heron?' I asked. 'It is very rough.'

'I am not afraid,' she told me calmly. 'I have done it once before, and Mary shall go with me.'

I did not say: but you were much younger then, and not ill, and in the company of your Husband. 'If you might delay, madam, while I conclude my business here, I should consider it an honour to accompany you, and offer you any such assistance along the way which you—and Mary—may need.'

Mrs Heron was quiet for a moment. 'Thank you, Mr Fox,' she said. 'That is kindly meant, and kindly taken. But how much longer shall you be here?'

'I do not know,' I admitted.

'I have been delaying this journey for twenty years,' she said. 'It is now time, and past time, that I go.'

'It must be difficult, to be leaving your husband behind,' I said.

Mrs Heron again did not respond directly, and when she did, she kept her head very still and very poised, looking straight ahead of her. 'Mr Heron will manage,' she said. 'It is difficult to leave Tam.'

'Could you not take him with you?'

'What place should he have in England?' she said.

We were an unlikely troupe. William O'Riordan was looking more and more dapper and refined the deeper into the streets of poverty we ventured, while the ill fit of my clothes grew more and more pronounced, with my trousers riding up my legs until they were bare to the knee like I were an overgrown schoolboy. Mrs Heron was waifish and brave, fluttering in the breeze, though half invisible, and Jack so like a Jack, so like any man you might see anywhere, it was difficult to remember he was there.

'I have seen the worst of all English words in print in this building,' he murmured to me, out of the hearing of Mrs Heron, as we went by a brick edifice with some pretensions to beauty rendered in dim and flaking plaster. 'A word I had never heard—I was young—but instinctively I knew upon sight, when an academic young whore tried to arouse my interest with a scandalous pamphlet from Sydney.'

Everything the man said sounded rehearsed to be clever.

As we passed the institution of the scandalous pamphlet, I slowed my pace to glance down the alleyway opening between it and its neighbouring hovel.

'What slows you?' asked Jack.

Together, we lagged behind as the others strode on.

'I believe I recognise that place,' I said.

'The alleyway?'

'Yes. It was very early morning, and I was in a state of some Confusion, but I do think that is where I bought my horse that was later stolen by somebody who I think was an agent of the horse-seller himself.'

We drew to a halt and looked down the alleyway. It was a dim place, even in the day-time, and reeked of all the dreadful substances one might imagine. Someone had scraped some vulgar remarks on the brothel wall in charcoal very low down, almost at ground level, as though ashamed.

'Why would you buy a horse in a such a place, and not expect deception?' Jack asked me. His polite tone indicated he asked neither to mock nor chastise, but merely for information. 'Was it your "state of Confusion"?'

'I do not know. It was foolish of me, I suppose. I was with William O'Riordan, who was acquainted with the horse-seller, and I suppose I was inclined to trust him. I did not think of questioning the proceedings, that is all.' I took a few halting steps into the shadow of the alley. 'I was quite glad that somebody was telling me what to do.'

'Come, Gabriel, let us go,' Jack said. 'This is not our purpose.'

I was only too pleased to step back into the light, although the odour of the place had already pasted itself thickly onto my skin.

'And you will come and meet my mother? Come and stay?' Jack asked me, as we hurried in pursuit of our group.

'You are very kind to invite me, but I should not wish to impose myself on her, if she is not expecting me,' I said.

'Well—yes, I do not know that she shall be expecting you, but Mrs Heron is coming, for they are of an age, and always liked one another, and it will be no trouble for you to come, too, for she—my mother—likes visitors. Especially visitors from England. You know my father died; you know that he founded the station, and then sold it to Heron, and then died. She has been alone ever since. You have given me the harpoons,' he said, talking over me a little, for he could see I was making another refusal. 'Let me offer you this.' And then, when I was silent, he added, 'I told Mr Heron you would go with me there,' and, finally, 'Where else shall you go?'

And so I accepted. There was a great comfort in having it settled, and having a place I could go, although I certainly did not know what to expect of Jack's mother.

'My mother is alone, as well,' I said.

'Your father also died? I am sorry to hear it.'

'No—he is alive, and they dwell in the same house. But she is quite friendless. Well—she has my brother, Freddie. But he has so little sway over domestic matters.'

A leaf of news-paper scurried across the street and flattened itself against a lamp-post. A bareheaded woman, her loose red hair pinned by the breeze to the air above her, smiled at me. Oh, dear God, I thought, if only some nice woman would come along, and take me apart, piece by piece, and wrap each limb in pages from the *Colonial Times*, and put my heart and other organs in her pockets, and pack my body parts in her basket, and take me in all my pieces home and make me into jugged man, and serve me to her friends with bread-and-butter!

'You have a faraway look in your eyes,' said William to me, turning to look at us as we drew near our party once again.

'Are you thinking of Mrs Cook?' asked Mrs Heron. She was setting a good, firm pace, her little boots very deftly avoiding all the most disgusting items upon the ground, her head high and her form neat, in radiant defiance of the slovenly types all around her, like the sublime young individual with the red hair.

I felt my blood rising and evaporating out of my skin.

A rat stopped to raise its eyebrows at me.

After Mamma and I had said goodbye to one another there in her attic-room, I turned away from her to face down the enormous Betty Sikes. This person was occupying the entire doorway, a gladiatorial set to her body, shaking her keys like some crude Christian-slaying weapon in order to hasten me to go, even while blocking my exit. I was compelled—not by Betty, but by some instinct—to look back and ask Mamma, in one of those moments of unreality when I could not quite believe what I was saying, 'Why did you marry him?'

'I was young, I suppose,' she said, looking out of the casement. 'It is nearly thirty years ago now, you know. And I imagine they told me what to do—to marry him. And I did not know him well.'

'He has always been unkind,' I said.

Mamma made a quick, dismissive movement with her hands. 'Not that so much,' she said. 'The difficulty is more that he has never understood that I am a person too.'

We both spoke quite slowly, calmly, in a light and conversational tone. 'Perhaps we ought to have talked of this sooner,' I said.

'What good would that have done?' she asked me.

I could not answer this. Should she have felt less solitary? Should I? I moved nearer her. Betty Sikes rattled her keys and heaved a great sigh from the doorway. I sat by Mamma on her little wooden bench, deliberately avoiding Betty's eye. 'Your life might have been quite different, if you had made a different choice then,' I said.

'That is true of all our lives, Gabriel,' she said, still looking away. 'They might always have been other than they are. It is of no use at all to anybody to regret one's past decisions.'

'Perhaps it is no use, and yet, it is quite natural to do, when one is—unhappy,' I said.

'True,' said she, finally turning her head, with what seemed to be an Herculean effort, to look at me. It was a shock to meet her eyes, as though we had until this point been occupying slightly different planes, and had now, finally, met. 'You look sad, my darling,' she said, resting her cold palm against my cheek for a moment.

I dropped my head and leant forward until I rested against her shoulder. How seldom I was touched by human hand!

She smoothed and smoothed my hair, her nervous movements reminding me very much of Freddie.

'Even so, I do not regret it,' she murmured. 'For how could I wish my children had never been born?'

'Well, I cannot speak to that, because I do not yet have children,' I said. 'Although I am glad to have life. But Father is so . . . well, I do not like to say it. But he is so very much that way.'

'Yes,' said Mamma. 'À *qui il a été beaucoup donné, il sera beaucoup demandé.*'

I straightened and made a literary sound of concurrence. Mamma knew I had done poorly at French. I suppose once my affectation of understanding may have made her smile, but not that day.

'It is something like: He to whom much is given, expects much,' she said.

'Yes, that is him.'

'Here is another for you,' she said. 'And you must look it up yourself, if you truly cannot understand me, although it is simpler than the first, and so I hope you might: *De qui je me fie Dieu me garde.*'

Cook's was a mean cottage amongst mean cottages, which made nothing of the sunshine, or the huge mountain hulking above us all, or the forest, or the sea—it was a house looking inwards towards itself, turning all other things out. The door was set wide open, for, I conjectured, what little sunlight the rosy dusk might now admit. We had all but Mrs Heron to stoop going in, that we might not hit our heads on the low lintel. Within it was as plain a place as one might imagine, but neatly and cleanly kept, swept and scrubbed. The hearth was the dominating fixture of the room, with a low fire flickering, and a pot hanging from one of two hooks above the flames, a low curl of steam falling from its lip. Before this was a girl seated at her mangle. Our shadows fell across her, but the firelight behind her lit her profile with a gentle brilliance. She sighed, and seemed to say something to herself, shook her head a little, and finally looked up at us. She was a slip of a thing, young, with ancient hands, and not even the faintest hint of the possibility that she might once have smiled, not even as a very little girl, before she knew of the world. Her hair was of no colour at all, and simply took on the colours of whatever was behind her, which, as she looked around at us, was now the fire, and now the brick, and now the raw stone wall. This hair was plaited tightly upon her head, but damp pieces had fallen down, which the baby bundled onto her back caught at. This, I supposed, was Mrs Cook. She turned and turned the handle of her mangle and fed the same red garment through the rollers over and again.

'Please do you step out of the sunlight,' she said to us. 'It is better if I can spare the candles.'

We arranged ourselves here and there from the doorway, and the sun fell across Mrs Cook once more. She winced a little, although it was not bright. Two more little children of indeterminate sex de-congealed themselves from the darkest corner and mutely presented themselves to their mother.

Mrs Heron stepped forwards, her husband's letter folded tightly in her hands.

Mrs Cook glanced at this. 'I cannot read,' she said. 'I have the ability, but not the luxury. Please read it to me.'

Another woman had slipped into the house behind us. She was somewhat older than Mrs Cook, and wore her hair under a mob cap, her bosom crossed with an apron. No one remarked upon her, so she said, 'I am a Neighbour,' and planted herself there in such a way that we understood her presence was Compulsory.

'Do you prefer your good Neighbour to take the children?' asked Mrs Heron.

'Not yet,' said Mrs Cook. 'Please, just read it to me.'

Mrs Heron began:

Dear Mrs Cook,
I am writing in order to fulfil a sad duty. I deeply regret to notify you of the accidental Death of your Husband, Edward Cook, which occurred during the diligent performance of his Duties upon the 13th day of July, 1842. I wish to convey my most heartfelt Condolences to you, and to your Family, and to place myself at your service in any matter in which I might be of some assistance.

Here Mrs Heron paused in order to peer at the young woman. Mrs Heron's voice had trembled as she read the letter aloud, but Mrs Cook sat on, her hands strong and unwavering in her work. Mrs Heron resumed:

> *I will endeavour to describe the Tragic Circumstances of that afternoon, that you might find some peace in the assurance of your late Husband's excellent conduct, and in the knowledge that those around him did not abandon him, but made an admirable attempt—*

'Please stop,' said Mrs Cook. The young wife—widow—was yet at her work, and gave no sign of having understood what Mrs Heron had read to her, except that copious quantities of Tears were flowing freely from her eyes and falling unchecked down her face. I had the thought that it was quite contrary to her work to be weeping such a flood, for she would soak the cloth.

'Where is he?' she asked.

'He is with friends, nearby, awaiting your wishes,' said Mrs Heron.

'Which friends?'

Mrs Heron gave the names of Mary and the men who remained with Cook's body.

'I do not know those people.'

'They are friends nevertheless, my dear.'

Mrs Cook had perhaps not been called Dear for some time, for she now commenced a quite visible battle against more tears. She pressed her face into the crook of her elbow for a moment, her hands slowing in their work.

'You will have to bring him here,' she told us, her voice muffled in her sleeve. 'If you would be so kind.'

'Yes, we shall bring him wherever you wish.'

She sighed and lifted her face to us once more. 'Yes—here. Bring him here, if you please,' she said, and then, 'Did you get the whale?—or was it lost?'

'We brought it in. If you should like, I shall read the rest of the letter to you, for it is not long, and you shall hear exactly what occurred.'

'No—please. No,' she said, her eyes upon her work. 'No. Leave the letter with me, please. Please do put it on the table.'

Mrs Heron did this.

'If you would be so kind,' said Mrs Cook, 'perhaps you might tell me in so many words what the letter says.'

'Of course I shall,' said Mrs Heron. 'Well, Mrs Cook, it recommends me to you, and introduces me as Mrs Heron, Mr Heron's wife, and exhorts you to make use of me, and that I will give you what comfort I might. And it introduces Mr O'Riordan and Mr Fox, who are here, and who tried to help preserve your husband's life. And it describes the Hunt on which Mr Cook died. And it offers Mr Heron's service, and his profoundest regrets, again, and asks you to please only apply to him for assistance, and he will give it, whatever it might be.'

Mrs Cook nodded.

'It says that Mr Cook exchanged poetical extracts with another man within the boat, and was in good cheer—'

'No!' she cried, her face contorted in sudden pain. 'Stop!' A trembling came upon her.

'What should you like us to do, my dear Mrs Cook?' Mrs Heron asked delicately, and edged nearer the girl, without touching her.

'I do not know!' she said fiercely. And then, 'What shall I do! Is there a commission?'

'Yes; included in the packet of Wages.'

'And that sum is everything?'

'Yes, that is all Mr Cook was owed, with the addition of—I hope you will forgive—a token sum towards his burial fees, and something for the children.' In fact, this sum was not at all token, and had been put there by Mr Heron, at the behest of the men, most of whom had taken the decision to give some proportion of their own commissions to the widow.

Mrs Cook looked at her two elder children. 'I will never fail them,' she said.

'I am sure you will not,' said Mrs Heron, drawing close. She stooped to press Mrs Cook's hands with her own, that she might stop working, and perhaps to quell the trembling. 'You strike me as a person of some fortitude.'

'I am paid for this,' said Mrs Cook, her face white and ghastly, pulling her hands away from Mrs Heron in order that she might gesture at the mangle. The tears had stopped. 'Pennies.'

As they conversed, the older child had come to a sad realisation. Its face broke like the cracking of an egg, and it began to cry most forlornly, which set off its younger siblings. Mrs Cook calmly rose and took her mangle and attempted to throw it against the wall, but it was too heavy, and so it merely toppled over with a very dull thud. She seemed that she might be taken by a swoon, for her head drooped on her thin neck, and she staggered dumbly forwards. The Neighbour sailed forth like a great Steamship and caught the young widow and steered her through a little door and into some dark place beyond.

'Now don't you go tearing at your hair and beating your breast in front of the children,' the Neighbour was saying. 'Let us go within, and you may have a good scream, and throw your fists about, but you must be composed when you come out again.'

Mrs Heron was drawn after them, and silence billowed after her. There was no screaming after all—none that we could hear, in any case. The two children left behind stopped crying and looked up at us, their mouths describing the shapes of Ripples upon the Water when a stone has been cast within, and their cheeks red, and great teardrops yet caught in their lower eyelashes. They looked from one of us to the other, and eventually presented themselves to Jack.

'There was once a king who had an ambitious brother,' said Jack, as we all stood looking down at the children who looked at us. 'The king was good and the brother was evil. What do you suppose the brother wanted?'

'To be the new king,' whispered the elder child, hiccuping through the words.

'Yes, that is correct. The evil brother wished to become the new king. What do you suppose he did?'

'He killed his brother.'

'No—for he was cowardly. Instead, he went into the castle dungeons, and stalked amongst the wretches chained therein, and found the most wretched wretch of all—this wretch was a creeping, cadaverous wretch, who had been sentenced to be chained to the dungeon wall for all his days until his dying breath—and when his dying breath was near, he was to be taken and beheaded—for he was a Murderer. He had hung there upon the dungeon wall for thirteen years and would have hung there for God only knows how much longer had the king's brother not come upon him. The king's brother—who was a Duke—had sentenced this Murderer himself, and when he had told the Murderer of his terrible fate, the Murderer had cast himself at the Duke's feet, and embraced his legs, and begged him for his Freedom, and said he would do anything to serve the Duke, if only he would have mercy. Of course, you and I know that the Duke did not have a merciful bone in his body, but he did have a good Nose for a deal, and when he found the Murderer in the dungeon, half mad with the Torture of Confinement, he said, "My friend, your time has come." And he leant into the stench of the man and whispered his terrible plot, and put an axe in his hand.

'The King slept with two guards outside his chambers, but in the peaceful Kingdom, under the auspices of the Good and Gentle King, the guards were entirely unprepared for any kind of incursion, and, when the Murderer came, disguised as a servant, and offered them food and wine, they ate and drank themselves into a stupor.'

'The Murderer had poisoned the wine and food,' the older child told Jack.

'You may be correct. In any case, the guards were sound asleep, and the Murderer crept past them, and into the King's bedchamber. The axe was very sharp, and the Murderer leapt upon the King's chest, and pressed the blade of the axe against his throat, and His Majesty awoke to the terrifying sight of the Murderer's yellow and rotten teeth bared in a terrible smile down at him!

"'King," said the Murderer. "I have been sent to kill you, for I have been promised my Freedom. But if you give me something greater, I shall spare you."

"'What greater thing is there than Freedom?" asked the King.

"'Why, money, of course, and a beautiful wife! Make me a Lord, and give me your daughter to marry, and I shall spare your life."

"'Yes, in that we are agreed—my child is more precious than Freedom," said the King. "I will not betray her. You might have riches, but you will never have my daughter." And so the Murderer chopped off his head.

'It was the Duke's scheme that the Murderer should chop up the King's body and feed him to the pigs. So the Murderer took his axe, and hacked the poor King's body into little pieces, and tied them all up in the blanket. But when he came to pick up the King's head and put it also in the blanket, it rolled away from him! And the Murderer made to seize it once more, and once more it rolled away! Every attempt the Murderer made to catch the head failed, for every time the head would shake from side to side and roll out of his grasp. The Murderer made a final lunge, and took the head, whose eyes were staring up at him, and it rolled again from side to side, and slipped out of his dreadful hands, and shouted and cried: "Murder! Murder!" And the guards awoke—'

'They were not poisoned,' said the elder child to the younger.

'They awoke, for they were not poisoned, and swooped in, and caught the Murderer, who confessed everything, and he and the Duke were sentenced to death, and were boiled alive the very next day. The King's daughter became a Queen, and ruled the kingdom for sixty years, doing very well by the Economy in her reign.

'And the moral of the story is: Uneasy lies the head that wears the Crown.'

Susannah's farewell had been subdued, which I hoped indicated love. Her face was half shadowed by her bonnet. She wore a dark watered silk which gave her the wild look of one just in from a storm. We shook hands very neatly, under the watchful eye of Mrs Prendergast, and the disapproving eye of my father.

'This child you are having my son find,' said Father to Mrs Prendergast. 'This Maginn girl.'

'She would be a child no longer, for she was sent away some thirty years ago,' said Mrs Prendergast.

'Very well. This—woman. She was sent as a convict?'

'Yes, Sir Alfred, she was.'

'And she is your Relative?'

'Yes, indeed. My Great-Niece.'

Father let the merest hint of a smile twitch the corners of his mouth. 'And you have not thought to seek her before now?'

'I have,' said the old lady. 'I have thought it many times.'

In the mean cottage of the Cook family, the Neighbour materialised from the inky dark of the far room. The baby was curled against her shoulder, evidently asleep, caught proficiently there by one great arm.

'How is Mrs Cook?' I asked.

'How do you think?' she snapped. 'She will have her husband's body brought here, at your convenience,' she told us, and left us once more for the depths of the cottage.

'Did the King wear his Crown to bed?' the younger child asked the elder, as we went away.

'No,' said the elder child. 'It is a Symbol.'

'I do not know what that means,' said the younger child.

'Perhaps neither do I.'

That is a sensible conclusion

THE MOST DISCREET METHOD WE could manage to transport Cook's body from the shipyard to his house was to parade in daylight's last fiery burst before night through the streets of Hobart-town with the whaleboat upon our shoulders and Cook laid out in state within. There were several carts at the shipyard, and I suggested we put Cook in one of these, and cover him respectfully with blankets, and wheel him to Mrs Cook's, but I was overruled unanimously. Mrs Heron had stayed behind with Mrs Cook, and so we walked, with Mary going ahead of us and the boat painfully upon our shoulders, and my ankles freezing, and my feet coming out of my moist boots, amongst the evening-crawlers of the town. We were neither stopped nor challenged, and the only person who paid us any attention was a tiny old man with a beard down to his knees, who asked us very politely what we were doing.

'Carrying our boat,' said Byrne, and the old man nodded and wandered away, his hands clasped professorially behind his back, and his beard rippling in the breeze.

I had not noticed the hill was so steep when we had first gone to the Cooks' house, but now, with our burden, I felt we were climbing a sheer cliff. By the time we arrived, my eyes were swimming, and my arms were certainly on fire.

Mary went into the house and brought Mrs Heron out to see. The latter lady gazed at us with eyes gone milky with sympathetic grief. 'Why did you bring the boat?' she asked.

'It was only right,' said Jack.

'It does not make any sense.'

Mrs Heron was a woman after my own heart, I thought, as we lowered the boat. 'Take his head,' said William to me. There was the sound of mud sucking from boots when I sank my fingers into the head of the shroud, and my hands came away thick with a clear slime. No one else seemed to notice this, and I became aware that it was not so, and there was no slime at all. I put my hands back upon the shroud, and helped carry him inside, as Pendle and Jack tipped the whaleboat against the side of the house.

'Are you still drunk?' William whispered to me.

'What? No!' I hissed in reply, and straightened my shoulders.

The children had gone, and so had the Neighbour, and the house seemed seven times larger with only the pale little matrons Cook and Heron within, and Mary, and a Priest of some description, who was smaller and paler still. Cook on the kitchen table, however, shrank the place back down again, until it seemed I could hardly move for the presence of the corpse.

We stood around with our hats off, awaiting the Priest's word, but he stood silent and with bowed head until Mrs Heron said, 'Very well, gentlemen. Thank you. You may go.'

'Will you not come with us?' said Jack to Mrs Heron.

'No. Mary and I shall remain here to-night, and sit up with Mrs Cook.'

'I cannot leave you here, madam,' he said.

Mrs Cook fired one red spark in each cheek. 'And why not?' she asked. 'Why cannot the lady stay here with me?'

And so, meekly, we departed. Pendle, Byrne and the Scot told us they were going to find whores. I thought of Maria Regina of the interesting black eyes, who had talked to me in such a frank and friendly way on my first night in the colony—a mere three nights ago! I hoped she had hung up her garters in the meantime, and found a nice man to marry, or had come into some money, and was sitting bundled safely by a kindly hearth somewhere, with a cat on her lap and a glass of sherry by her side. I put her into that pleasant reality in my mind, and kept her there. And my mind slipped from that scene to my mother in her cold attic-room, quite alone, and Trapped, a decaying old carpet under her feet. And then I thought back to Maria Regina strolling easily up to me in the tap-room, plump and vivacious, giving no indication she was not perfectly content with her life as it was.

We lingered on the muddy corner by the Cooks' house. Pendle, Byrne and the Scot were gone, and William looked after them, and said he might go to the Cock and Bale, and rest himself by the great hearth there, and ponder things over a jug of wine. 'Come with me, if you like, Fox,' he said to me.

'Thank you; that is a kind invitation, but I must offer my regrets, for I have already accepted an invitation to Jack's mother's place,' I said, feeling immensely awkward. Jack inclined his head. My wet clothes, bundled as they were, hung heavily from my hand.

'Ah, yes,' said William.

'Shall we meet again?'

'I do not know,' he said, with a smile. 'It is you who are the proponent of Fate. What say you?'

'Yes, I hope so. I have been glad of your company.'

'I have been glad of yours.'

'I must confess something to you, William,' I said, taking a steadying breath.

'What is it, Gabriel?' he said with an air of good-natured mockery.

'I thought you a Cannibal, when first I met you.'

William started. 'Why?'

'Because you have bad teeth, and are Irish,' I said simply. 'Please forgive me.' The words hung in the air a moment before whispering away.

'Well!—you amaze me rather. I cannot forgive you for calling my teeth bad, when yours are like an old woman's fingernails. But you are English, and so your ignorance is only to be expected. But why—why a Cannibal, Gabriel? The Irish are called many things, but I did not know we were thought of thus.'

'I had some bad advice, and I am very sorry that I listened to it.'

'There was a Cannibal Irishman here, some years back,' William conceded. 'He had stolen some boots back in Ireland, that is why he was here. But he was not the only Cannibal in his party, and he did keep company with some English, as well as Irish. So if I am a Cannibal on the strength of that, then so too are you, my friend. And now, I go to the Cock and Bale, to drink, sup, and rest. And to buy a jug of wine to take back to the station for my father, who very seldom has wine.'

'I am a Cannibal,' said Jack.

'You are droll,' said William.

'Why is your father here?' I asked him.

'He was transported—so I followed him, that he would have a friend.'

My mother sat at the garret window, not looking at me.

'William, I do not quite understand you,' I said.

'Do you mean generally, or specifically in this instance, about the wine, and my father?'

'Generally, I think.'

'That is simply as it is. In fact—nor do I quite understand you.'

'William—'

'Yes? Gabriel, it is cold, and will only grow colder, the longer we stand here.'

'Yes—please—I shall not detain you very much longer. Only tell me where I might find that German man who sold me Tigris. I should like to find her again and have her back. Should he be near the alleyway in which we conducted our business?'

'Perhaps. Why do you wish to find that horse? She was not an extremely remarkable Creature.'

'No, but she is mine, I suppose, and I did grow fond of her, and she bore me patiently enough.'

'I do not believe she is yours any longer,' he said.

'Who is Tigris?' asked Jack.

'The horse that I bought and was stolen from me,' I said.

'Or: the stolen horse that he rented and that was stolen back,' said William.

'Odd name,' said Jack.

'No,' said William. 'The Tigris River, a tributary of Lake Hazar, in Turkey. Come, Jack, you were schooled somewhere or other, were you not? Tigris and her sire were Turkoman.'

'William O'Riordan, your learned remark reminds me that once you told me you speak French,' I said. 'May I ask you a question about it?'

William threw his hands up in an attitude of despair. 'Very well. I surrender. You might ask whatever you wish, but Gabriel, you do have so very many questions for me! Come, let us walk in the direction of the Cock and Bale, at least, and warm ourselves by the exercise. Or we might walk towards your lady mother's house, Jack—I do not care. Let us go.'

And so we set off together, downhill, in what I thought was the direction of the water.

'I do. I have nothing but questions, and not only for you. In this case, I fear I rather misused my French tutor, and did not learn well when he tried to teach me. Not even holidays in the South of France could drill it into my thick head, for everybody speaks English there anyway. Will you make a translation for me?'

'You insult my teeth, and are ignorant about my country and my countrymen, and then ask me a favour?' He was unsmiling, but he spoke gently, and his eyes were kind.

'I am sorry, William.'

'How long will it take?'

'No time at all—it is a line only. *De qui je me fie Dieu me garde.*'

'Oh, that is a proverb,' he said, with a dismissive gesture. 'Its substance is something like, God guard me from those I trust.'

I offered my hand, and he wrapped his arms around me, and kissed my cheek, and when he released me, he left a cold place in my own arms where he had stood. 'Silly man,' he said.

'He is most certainly a Communist,' said Jack, watching him go away.

'I truly do not know what that means.'

On my first night in Van Diemen's Land, I had met William. On my second night, I had walked alone into the station, harpoons over my shoulder. And on the third, I had sat at a table with Mr and Mrs Heron as they told me of the end of all their dreams. And now, on the fourth night, I was shown by a girl with a Welsh look about her into the third-grandest house in a colony of no truly grand houses, wearing a set of clothes that was shrinking by the minute. Jack and I were put into a drawing-room, and were seated on velvet chairs, and offered port and biscuits, by that same tidy young miss. I did not wish to put my bundle down, for it was still damp, and she took it from me, and told me she would hang my things before the kitchen-fire, and get them nice and dry for me.

'They shall be stiff as boards when she brings them back,' Jack told me. As he sipped from his dainty glass, telling me a little about the Artworks hanging upon the walls, I saw for the first time just how out-of-place that young man was at the station, out in the freezing cold, harpooning whales. There were dainties and doilies and covers and cosies neatly put upon every surface in that room. Looming above us upon several walls were great glowing oil paintings, and strange little handiworks displayed here and there—every sign, in short, of a respectably idle life. Jack himself, though younger and handsomer, gazed down at me from a painting hung above the mantelpiece. He looked to be not yet one-and-twenty in the picture, and sat with his hand upon an harpoon.

The flesh Jack arose to take down a small wooden frame from the wall and to bring it to me, that I might admire his mother's work of arranging dead moths into precisely geometric forms. I had reached deep within myself to muster some faint shadow of approbation for that item when I was compelled to rise to my feet, for a tall and slender lady entered the room, holding her arms open to Jack. I felt the seams of my ill-fitting costume creak and strain as I rose to my feet.

It was some quirk of Nature I had not seen before that made the grown son shorter than the mother, but other than that odd discrepancy, Jack and Mrs Montserrat were very alike. She had his hazel eyes—rather, I suppose, he had hers—and chestnut hair, though hers was rather greyer than his.

When Jack presented me to this lady, she pressed my hand warmly for a moment, and bade me be seated once more. She was polished in a way I did not even realise I had missed until I met her, and her charmingly easy and sociable manner, in her well-appointed house, brought the spectre of my mother before me so strongly I found I had to rise and make an agitated lap around the room in order to prevent myself from screaming and shouting, or committing some act of violence against the dead moths in their little frame.

'I met Mr Fox at the station, Mamma,' said Jack. 'He brought me a pair of American harpoons as a trade.'

'I am sure they were very interesting, but my poor head cannot really handle the matter of harpoons,' said Mrs Montserrat.

'You are telling me I am boring you,' said Jack with a smile.

'Not quite—are you in the harpooning business, Mr Fox?' she asked me.

'No, madam, I am not. I came upon them by circumstance, and had some information that I might sell them at Montserrat Station, for I was having some trouble divesting myself of them.'

'And, instead of selling, you traded them with my son?'

'Jack has kindly indicated that I might keep the costume I am wearing, which he gave me when my own became too wet to wear.'

'Oh, you poor man, Mr Fox! His things are tiny on you!'

'Thank you, yes. Thus, although I am most profoundly grateful, Jack, I shall consider these clothes a loan, and return them to you—for they do not fit me, truly. I have been going about half bare—forgive me, madam!' I said, but she was unperturbed at the mention of unclothed flesh. 'And therefore, Jack, I give you the harpoons. Please accept them as a gift, for I have but little to give, and wish to give something.'

'I thank you, and although you are most heartily welcome to keep the clothing, I can see that it does not fit you well. But I must say—did you not pay attention to O'Riordan?' Jack asked me. 'You cannot give them to me, for you are participant in a convoluted system of Harmonic Exchange.'

'Oh—yes, he did say something to that effect.'

'Therefore, we can trust that you will receive something in return for the irons.'

'If you ascribe to his conceit, which I do not.'

'You ought,' said Jack.

'It is refreshing that you two young people are so charmingly familiar with one another, so soon in your acquaintance,' said Mrs Montserrat, and I could not divine if she were truly refreshed, or if she were making a pointed remark of some kind. I had never yet plumbed the politics of the human Heart, particularly in that place, where everybody's intentions were slightly unavailable to me. Mrs Montserrat could clearly hear my thoughts echoing in my own head, for she smiled very graciously at me and said, 'He who can describe how his heart is ablaze is burning on a small pyre,' which I gathered was some quotation or other. Mamma was also fond of quotations, adages, couplets and other such little lines, often producing them at the pertinent point in conversation, or noting them in her diary. Thinking of this, I was struck by a sharp pain, as real as any pain with a physical cause, in my chest.

Mamma had constantly kept a diary before she was put away. There was a full shelf of these in the library: little leather-bound volumes brimming with words of consequence to her, all looping across the pages in her elegant hand. Each entry began with the date, and the day, and the weather, and would continue on to detail all her comings-and-goings since the previous day. She wrote a great deal about my brothers and me, such that reading the diaries she had kept when I was a young child was like lifting a heavy stone and finding beneath it the ground seething and boiling with hidden beetles. How many things did I come upon in those volumes that gave me a start of familiarity, and the sudden re-introduction of a memory I had not known I possessed?

> *Saturday, the twenty-fifth of March in the year 1820. It rained in the night, and there was a frost this morning, but then the sun came out and it was passing fine. With my morning letters, I received word from Alfred that he should remain away some little time longer than he had at first intended. Later, I received Lady F. and Miss F., Mrs P., the Misses H. The visiting-hour was drawing to its close when the Misses H. were here, and we are quite informal together, and so we took together a turn about the rose-garden. There we came across Freddie and Gabriel tucked behind the old wall bordering the southern end. Freddie had removed not only both shoes but also his socks, in order that he might put these items over his hands, and amuse Gabriel with a little puppet-show of two sock-creatures who seemed to wish nothing more than to make little Gabriel their King. He was much delighted with this display—indeed, they both were. We crept away that we would not disturb them at their play. I am glad it was the Misses H. with me to witness this; Lady F. is quite old-fashioned about*

her own children, and I do not yet know what Mrs P. would make of such a funny thing.

I had never understood this need in her, to maintain her writing so thoroughly, and so unfailingly, over the years, that her thoughts and doings might be preserved. Well, perhaps I had understood, from an observer's point of view, but I had been unable to take up the practice myself. I had tried! How can the intangible artefacts of life ever faithfully be recorded? Probably I simply lack the skill, but how could I—for example—reproduce perfectly enough the shades of occurrence and meaning of the many occasions in my childhood when John would insist I was upset when I was not, and so I would become upset, and he would be satisfied, and laugh at my red face? How could I put into words those emotions, and the tiny flickers of cold-hearted intent in John? Or the shifting quality in Mamma's eye—partly sad, partly amused, and partly some other thing—when she would look at me in solidarity as Father made some particularly imperious remark? How Freddie and I would dash through the beech wood for sheer joy, and it would be understood between us that the joy was fleeting, and that we must soon return indoors, and that understanding only made us whoop louder, and run faster? Or how, when Susannah told me her mother had been Welsh, and I'd said, 'Oh, they love Leeks there, do they not?' and she had supressed a smile at my silly remark that nevertheless reached her eyes? I can write the words, but they seem hollow and impotent! And the memories themselves are quite hazy. It is like I have told myself the story of the memory, and I am remembering the story—and not the thing itself.

It seemed so impossible that I sometimes felt within myself a deep yearning to be forgotten entirely. I should have liked to be painted out of the portraits, to be struck from Mamma's diaries while I was still living, and to be set free somewhere wild and strange.

Of course, for the first time in my five-and-twenty years, I was indeed somewhere wild and strange. And yet I found I did not feel the anonymous liberation of my dreams. I knew that, far away at Home, my portrait frowned over the quiet Hall, and Mamma's memories of me were stained into the pages arrayed there on the library shelf for any idle hand to take up.

The lady duly invited us to dine, and Jack indicated that he would withdraw to dress.

'Take Mr Fox, surely,' said Mrs Montserrat. 'He must be in some discomfort in your things.'

I made all the proper protestations, assuring both, though neither was listening, that I was quite comfortable, and the sausage-skin clothing was most commodious, and that therefore there was no need for anybody to trouble themselves about me.

'Come, Mr Fox,' said Jack, calmly cutting through my polite explanations.

Jack did find me a better-fitting suit—rather, he sent a servant to find me one—which he told me was his father's. Therefore, it was outdated, dusty and morbid.

Although our meal was informal, it was the first occasion I had really dined since Sydney-town. Mrs Montserrat presided over our repast, which was served competently, but without excess ceremony, by a nicely attired young manservant. The wine was good—proper wine—and we ate brown soup, fish in a white sauce, beef with mushrooms done some clever way in cream, and a suet pudding with custard. Proper food!

'I beg your indulgence for the simplicity of our table, Mr Fox,' said Mrs Montserrat. 'You are no doubt accustomed to something rather more refined.'

'Oh, madam,' I said. 'Lately I find I have become accustomed to hardships I had never dreamt of, and thus your table is a fabled Cornucopia to me now.' She smiled modestly, and I hurriedly added, 'Of course, Mrs Montserrat, even had I suffered no hardship, I should still be very happy to be here . . .'

'You are kind,' she said. 'And where are your people?'

'Norfolk, mostly,' I said, and I named our native village.

'Oh, you are *those* Foxes,' she said. 'That is good. I grew up quite near that place. What are your parents called?'

I was charmed by the unpretentiousness of this question, and of the lady herself, I must say. 'They are Sir Alfred and Lady Fox,' I said, and from that simple nicety, I found I could not but expound upon the whole sorry tale of my mother, to one so kindly listening as Mrs Montserrat. I told her how Mamma had fallen out of fashion amongst her circle, and had grown sad—or had grown sad and then fallen out of fashion as a result; I did not know—and I found myself even disclosing the private shame of her outburst on Christmas Day, and her subsequent locking-up. What daze had come upon me, that I should say so freely such frank and intimate things!

'That is a very grave thing,' said Mrs Montserrat.

'It is,' I replied, wishing I had not told her of it. I attempted a discreet change of topic, which I handled with all the subtlety of a frigate in a fishpond. 'And what brought you to the colonies?' I asked. 'Did you accompany your husband?'

'No, for I met him here,' she said. 'How long has your mother been put away?'

I told her that it had been since Boxing Day.

She inclined her head in a very subdued manner. 'You are unmarried, I think,' she said.

So I described Susannah, and gave a few details of what had gone between us. As I was speaking, however, and when I begged leave to pass over the miniature for her to admire, I thought of the matter of Susannah's grey eyes, and how she had refused me, and not spoken to me ever again, except for an excessively courteous farewell. I found myself saying that perhaps she was not the girl for me.

'That is a sensible conclusion,' Mrs Montserrat said, and gave me back the painting.

'Thank you,' I said.

'But Susannah has a Relative,' said Jack.

'Most girls do,' said his mother.

'This one was a Lady at great advantage, in pecuniary terms, and those of Years.'

'A rich old lady,' said his mother, smiling now.

'Yes—Mrs Prendergast,' I said. 'There is a woman, somewhere, here, in Van Diemen's Land, unless she had died or otherwise departed, called Maryanne Maginn. Mrs Prendergast gave me a letter to put into Maryanne Maginn's hands, and a letter of credit, which gave me access to a great deal of money, with which to live, and support myself, and bring us both Home, after I had found her. Both of these things are now gone—the Letter, and the Money. And I find myself somewhat at a loss.'

'Why at a loss?' asked Mrs Montserrat.

'Well, because I fear I do not know quite what to do next. That is, I have determined that I must find some kind of work, and raise some money, and continue my search for Maryanne Maginn, as I have promised. But I do not yet know how I shall go about this.'

'Well—yes: that is one path of many you might choose. Do consider, however, that you need not decide hastily, nor think you are not Free to choose differently.'

'You are right, Madam, of course,' I said. 'I might also consider that I write to Mrs Prendergast, and have her send another letter of credit, and continue my search thus equipped, and thus forgo the need to secure paid employment. For that, of course, I should have to admit that I had been careless with the letters she had entrusted to me.'

'Yes; alternatively, you might free yourself of Mrs Prendergast, and go on with your own life, and leave Maryanne Maginn to hers.'

'Ah—with regards to that, Madam, I do not know that I am free to so do. I have given my solemnest vow to Mrs Prendergast that I should certainly find Miss Maginn.'

'Perhaps your Miss Maginn has a life of her own, and does not need to be found,' said Mrs Montserrat.

'I suppose that could be true.'

'She might have changed her name.'

'Yes, she might have married.'

'And your Mrs Prendergast felt sure she would wish to go Home?'

'Yes—she did not doubt it.'

'Do you know what was in the letter she wrote?'

'No! Madam, I certainly did not read it.'

'You do not know if it was apology, or the opposite—forgiveness?'

'Is forgiveness the opposite of apology? Is it not blame?'

'It does not matter, Mr Fox.'

'An academic point merely.'

'Perhaps.' She paused. 'You ought to go Home,' she said. 'You must see to your own family.'

'I do not think Susannah will accept me,' I said. 'I think . . . I have thought a great deal of this matter, lately. And I have concluded that, if she has refused me, as she has, then that must be the last word on the matter. Unless she decides to give me some reason to hope. But I am better served if I do not wait for that signal of hope. I truly feel that I have let her go in my heart—well, not my feeling for her, perhaps, but my feeling that I have a claim on her—just in the course of a few days!'

Mrs Montserrat responded to this, which was a frankly outrageous outburst before near strangers, very simply. 'That is not the family to which I refer,' she said. And a picture of my mother arose again between us.

I looked down at my place and collected my thoughts. 'I wish that I had completed my task,' I said, after a pause. 'I only feel ashamed that I did not take better care of the letter Mrs Prendergast wrote. It was a precious thing, and it did not belong to me, and I did not pay it a moment's thought when I went out upon the water with it in my pocket.'

'I think you can be forgiven that, at least,' said Mrs Montserrat. 'You could not have known you would go into the water. And, if I am quite frank with you, even if you had preserved the letter, and had given it to me, I should not have bothered to read it.'